LLOYD C. DOUGLAS

The Robe

LONDON: PETER DAVIES

Dedicated with appreciation
to
HAZEL McCANN
who wondered what became of
The Robe

FIRST PUBLISHED MAY 1943
REPRINTED MARCH 1944
REPRINTED MAY 1945
REPRINTED JUNE 1946
REPRINTED SEPTEMBER 1946
REPRINTED JANUARY 1947
REPRINTED MAY 1947
REPRINTED OCTOBER 1947
REPRINTED FEBRUARY 1948
REPRINTED JULY 1948
REPRINTED JANUARY 1949
REPRINTED MAY 1949
REPRINTED SEPTEMBER 1949
REPRINTED (RESET) SEPTEMBER 1950
REPRINTED OCTOBER 1952
REPRINTED OCTOBER 1953
REPRINTED NOVEMBER 1953
REPRINTED MARCH 1954

MADE AND PRINTED IN GREAT BRITAIN FOR PETER DAVIES LIMITED
BY WILLIAM CLOWES AND SONS LIMITED
LONDON AND BECCLES

Chapter I

BECAUSE she was only fifteen and busy with her growing up, Lucia's periods of reflection were brief and infrequent; but this morning she felt weighted with responsibility.

Last night her mother, who rarely talked to her about anything more perplexing than the advantages of clean hands and a pure heart, had privately discussed the possible outcome of Father's reckless remarks yesterday in the Senate; and Lucia, flattered by this confidence, had declared maturely that Prince Gaius wasn't in a position to do anything about it.

But after she had gone to bed, Lucia began to fret. Gaius might indeed overlook her father's heated comments about the extravagances and mismanagement of his government, if he had had no previous occasion for grievance against the Gallio family. There was, however, another grievance that no one knew about except herself—and Diana. They would all have to be careful now or they might get into serious trouble.

The birds had awakened her early. She was not yet used to their flutterings and twitterings, for they had returned much sooner than usual, Spring having arrived and unpacked before February's lease was up. Lucia roused to a consciousness of the fret that she had taken to bed with her. It was still there, like a toothache.

Dressing quietly so as not to disturb Tertia, who was soundly sleeping in the alcove—and would be alarmed when she roused to find her mistress's couch vacant—Lucia slipped her sandals softly over the exquisitely wrought mosaics that led from her bedchamber and through her parlour into the long corridor and down the wide stairway to the spacious hall and out into the vast peristyle, where she paused, shielding her eyes against the sun.

For the past year or more, Lucia had been acutely conscious of her increasing height and rapid development into womanhood; but here on this expanse of tessellated tiling she always felt very insignificant. Everything in this immense peristyle dwarfed her: the tall marble columns that supported the vaulted roofs, the stately statues standing in their silent dignity on the close-clipped lawn, the high silvery spray of the fountain. No matter how old she became, she would be ever a child here.

Nor did it make her feel any more mature when, proceeding along the patterned pavement, she passed Servius, whose face had been as bronzed and deep-lined when Lucia was a mere toddler. Acknowledging with twinkling fingers and a smile the old slave's grave salute, as he brought the shaft of his spear to his wrinkled forehead, she moved on to the vine-covered pergola at the far end of the rectangle.

There, with her folded arms resting on the marble balustrade that overlooked the terraced gardens, the arbours, the tiled pool, and commanded a breath-taking view of the city and the river, Lucia tried to decide whether to tell Marcellus. He would be terrifically angry, of course, and if he did anything about it at all he might make matters worse; but—somebody in the family must be informed where we stood in the opinion of Gaius before any more risks were taken. It was unlikely, thought Lucia, that she would have an opportunity to talk alone with her brother until later in the day; for Marcellus had been out—probably all night—at the Military Tribunes' banquet, and wouldn't be up before noon; but she must resolve at once upon a course of action. She wished now that she had told Marcellus last summer, when it had happened.

The soft whisper of sandal-straps made her turn about. Decimus the butler was approaching, followed by the Macedonian twins bearing silver trays held aloft on their outspread palms. Would his mistress, inquired Decimus with a deep bow, desire her breakfast served here?

'Why not?' said Lucia, absently.

Decimus barked at the twins and they made haste to prepare the table, while Lucia watched their graceful movements with amused curiosity, as if observing the antics of a pair of playful terriers. Pretty things, they were; a little older than she, though not so tall; agile and shapely, and as nearly alike as two peas. It was the first time that Lucia had seen them in action, for they had been purchased only a week ago. Apparently Decimus, who had been training them, thought they were ready now for active duty. It would be interesting to see how they performed, for her father said they had been brought up in a home of refinement and were probably having their first experience of serving a table. Without risking an inquiring glance at the young woman who stood watching them, they proceeded swiftly but quietly with their task. They were both very pale, Lucia observed, doubtless from confinement in some prison-ship.

One of Father's hobbies, and his chief extravagance, was the possession of valuable slaves. The Gallio family did not own very many, for Father considered it a vulgar, dangerous, and ruinously expensive vanity to have swarms of them about with little to do but eat, sulk, and conspire. He selected his slaves with the same discriminating care that he exercised when purchasing beautiful statuary and other art objects. He had no interest in public sales. Upon the return of a military expedition from some civilized country, the commanding officers would notify a few of their well-to-do acquaintances that a limited number of high-grade captives were available; and Father would go down, the day before the sale, and look them over, learn their history, sound them out, and if he found anything he wanted to add to his household staff he would bid. He never told anyone in the family how much he had paid for their slaves, but it was generally felt that he had never practised economy in acquiring such merchandise.

Most of the people they knew were in a constant dither about their slaves; buying and selling and enchanging. It wasn't often that her father disposed of one; and when, rarely, he had done so, it was because the slave had mistreated another over whom he had some small authority. They had lost an excellent cook that way, about a year ago. Minna had grown crusty and cruel toward the kitchen crew, scolding them loudly and knocking them about. She had been warned a few times. Then, one day, Minna had slapped Tertia. Lucia wondered, briefly, where Minna was now. She certainly did know how to bake honey cakes.

You had to say this for Father: he was a good judge of people. Of course, slaves weren't people, exactly; but some of them were almost people. There was Demetrius, for example, who was at this moment marching through the colonnade with long, measured strides. Father had bought Demetrius six years ago and presented him to Marcellus on his seventeenth birthday. What a wonderful day that was, with all their good friends assembled in the Forum to see Marcellus—clean-shaven for the first time in his life—step forward to receive his white toga. Cornelius Capito and Father had made speeches, and then they had put the white toga on Marcellus. Lucia had been so proud and happy that her heart had pounded and her throat had hurt, though she was only nine then, and couldn't know much about the ceremony except that Marcellus was expected to act like a man now—though sometimes he forgot to, when Demetrius wasn't about.

Lucia pursed her full lips and grinned as she thought of their relationship: Demetrius, two years older than Marcellus, always so seriously respectful, never relaxing for an instant from his position as a slave; Marcellus, stern and dignified, but occasionally forgetting to be the master and slipping absurdly into the role of intimate friend. Very funny it was sometimes. Lucia loved to watch them together at such moments. Of course she had about the same relation to Tertia; but that seemed different.

Demetrius had come from Corinth, where his father (a wealthy shipowner) had taken a too conspicuous part in defensive politics.

Everything had happened at once in Demetrius's family. His father had been executed, his two elder brothers had been given to the new Legate of Achaea, his patrician mother had committed suicide; and Demetrius—tall, handsome, athletic—had been brought to Rome under heavy guard, for he was not only valuable but violent.

Lucia remembered when, a week before Marcellus's coming of age, she had heard Father telling Mother about his purchase of the Corinthian slave, only an hour earlier. She had been much impressed—and a little frightened, too.

'He will require careful handling for a while,' her father was saying. 'He has seen some rough treatment. His keeper told me I had better sleep with a dagger under my pillow until the Corinthian cooled down. It seems he had badly beaten up one of his guards. Ordinarily, of course, they would have dealt with him briefly and decisively; but they were under orders to deliver him uninjured. They were quite relieved to get him off their hands.'

'But is this not dangerous?' her mother had inquired anxiously. 'What might he not do to our son?'

'That,' Father had replied, 'will depend on Marcellus. He will have to win the fellow's loyalty. And he can do it, I think. All that Demetrius needs is an assurance of fair play. He will not expect to be petted. He is a slave, and he knows it—and hates it; but he will respond to decent discipline.' And then he had gone on to say that after he had paid the money and signed the documents, he had himself led Demetrius out of the narrow cell; and, when they were in the open plaza, had unlocked his chains; very carefully, too, for his wrists were raw and bleeding. 'Then I walked on ahead of him,' he had continued, 'without turning to see whether he was following me. Aulus had driven me down and was waiting in the chariot at the Appian Gate, a few yards away. I had planned to bring the Corinthian back with me. But, as we neared the chariot, I decided to give him instructions about how to reach our villa on foot.'

'Alone?' Mother had exclaimed. 'Was that not very risky?'

'Yes,' Father had agreed, 'but not quite so risky as to have brought him here as a shackled prisoner. He was free to run away. I wanted him to be in a position to decide whether he would rather take a chance with us than gamble on some other fate. I could see that my gestures of confidence had surprised and mellowed him a little. He said—in beautiful Greek, for he had been well educated— "What shall I do, sir, when I arrive at your villa?" I told him to inquire for Marcipor, who would advise him. He nodded, and stood fumbling with the rusty chains that I had loosed from his hands.

"Throw them away," I said. Then I mounted the chariot, and drove home.'

'I wonder if you will ever see him again,' Mother had said; and, in answer to her question, Marcipor appeared in the doorway.

'A young Corinthian has arrived, Master,' said Marcipor, a Corinthian himself. 'He says he belongs to us.'

'That is true,' Father said, pleased with the news. 'I bought him this morning. He will attend my son, though Marcellus is to know nothing of this for the present. Feed him well. And provide him with a bath and clean clothing. He has been imprisoned for a long time.'

'The Greek has already bathed, Master,' replied Marcipor.

'Quite right. That was thoughtful of you.'

'I had not yet thought of it,' admitted Marcipor. 'I was in the sunken garden, supervising the building of the new rose arbour, when this Greek appeared. Having told me his name, and that he belonged here, he caught sight of the pool——'

'You mean,' expostulated Mother, 'that he dared to use our pool?'

'I am sorry,' Marcipor replied. 'It happened so quickly I was unable to thwart him. He ran swiftly, tossing aside his garments, and dived in. I regret the incident. The pool will be drained immediately and thoroughly cleansed.'

'Very good, Marcipor,' said Father. 'And do not rebuke him; though he should be advised not to do that again.' And he had laughed, after Marcipor had left the room. Mother said, 'The fellow should have known better than that.' 'Doubtless he did,' Father had replied. 'But I cannot blame him. He must have been extremely dirty. The sight of that much water probably drove him temporarily insane.'

One could be sure, reflected Lucia, that Marcipor hadn't been too hard on poor Demetrius; for, from that day, he had treated him as if he were his own son. Indeed, the attachment was so close that slaves more recently acquired often asked if Marcipor and Demetrius were not somehow related.

*   *   *   *   *   *

Demetrius had reappeared from the house now, and was advancing over the tiled pavement on his way to the pergola. Lucia wondered what errand was bringing him. Presently he was standing before her, waiting for a signal to speak.

'Yes, Demetrius?' she drawled.

'The Tribune,' he announced, with dignity, 'presents his good wishes for his sister's health and happiness, and requests that he be permitted to join her at breakfast.'

1 *

Lucia brightened momentarily; then sobered, and replied, 'Inform your master that his sister will be much pleased—and tell him,' she added, in a tone somewhat less formal, 'that breakfast will be served here in the pergola.'

After Demetrius had bowed deeply and was turning to go, Lucia sauntered past him and proceeded along the pavement for several yards. He followed her at a discreet distance. When they were out of earshot, she paused and confronted him.

'How does he happen to be up so early?' she asked, in a tone that invited frankness. 'Didn't he go to the banquet?'

'The Tribune attended the banquet,' replied Demetrius, respectfully. 'It is of that, perhaps, that he is impatient to speak.'

'Now don't tell me that he got into some sort of mess, Demetrius.' She tried to invade his eyes, but the bridge was up.

'If so,' he replied, prudently, 'the Tribune may wish to report it without the assistance of his slave. Shall I go now ?'

'You were there, of course, attending my brother,' pursued Lucia. And when Demetrius bowed an affirmative, she asked, 'Was Prince Gaius there?' Demetrius bowed again, and she went on, uncertainly, 'Did you—was he—had you an opportunity to notice whether the Prince was in a good humour?'

'Very,' replied Demetrius, 'until he went to sleep.'

'Drunk?'   Lucia wrinkled her nose.

'It is possible,' deliberated Demetrius, 'but it is not for me to say.'

'Did the Prince seem friendly—toward my brother?' persisted Lucia.

'No more than usual.'   Demetrius shifted his weight and glanced toward the house.

Lucia sighed significantly, shook her black curls, and pouted. 'You can be very trying sometimes, Demetrius.'

'I know,' he admitted, ruefully. 'May I go now? My master——'

'By all means!' snapped Lucia. 'And swiftly!'   She turned and marched back with clipped steps to the pergola. Something had gone wrong last night, or Demetrius wouldn't have taken up that frozen attitude.

Decimus, whose instinct advised him that his young mistress was displeased, retreated to a safe distance. The twins, who had now finished laying the table, were standing side by side awaiting orders. Lucia advanced on them.

'What are you called?' she demanded, her tone still showing annoyance.

'I am Helen,' squeaked one of them, nervously. 'My sister is Nesta.'

'Can't she talk?'

'Please—she is frightened.'

Their long-lashed eyes widened with apprehension as Lucia drew closer, but they did not flinch. Cupping her hands softly under their round chins, she drew up their faces, smiled a little, and said, 'Don't be afraid. I won't bite you.' Then—as if caressing a doll—she toyed with the tight little curls that had escaped from Helen's cap. Turning to Nesta, she untied and painstakingly retied her broad sash. Both girls' eyes were swimming. Nesta stopped a big tear with the back of her hand.

'Now, now,' soothed Lucia, 'don't cry. No one is going to hurt you here.' She impulsively abandoned the lullaby, drew herself erect, and declared proudly, 'You belong to Senator Marcus Lucan Gallio! He paid a great price for you—because you are valuable; and—because you are valuable—you will not be mistreated. . . . Decimus,' she called, over her shoulder, 'see that these pretty children have new tunics; white ones, with coral trimmings.' She picked up their hands, one by one, and examined them critically. 'Clean,' she remarked, half aloud, 'and beautiful, too. That is good.' Facing Decimus, she said, ' You may go now. Take the twins. Let them bring the food. My brother will have breakfast with me here. You need not come back.'

Lucia had never liked Decimus very well; not that there was any particular ground for complaint, for he was a perfect servant; almost too deferential, with a chilling deference that lacked only a little of being sulkiness. It had been Lucia's observation that imported slaves were more comfortable to live with than the natives. Decimus had been born in Rome and had been in their family for almost as long as Lucia could remember. He had a responsible position; attended to all the purchasing of supplies for their tables, personally interviewed the merchants, visited the markets, met the foreign caravans that brought spices and other exotics from afar; a very competent person indeed, who minded his own business, kept his own counsel, and carried himself with dignity. But he was a stranger.

One never could feel towards Decimus as one did toward good old Marcipor, who was always so gentle—and trustworthy too. Marcipor had managed the business affairs of the family for so long that he probably knew more about their estate than Father did.

Decimus bowed gravely now, as Lucia dismissed him, and started toward the house, his stiff back registering disapproval of this episode that had flouted the discipline he believed in and firmly exercised. The Macedonians, their small even teeth flashing an ecstatic smile, scampered away, hand in hand, without waiting for formal permission. Lucia stopped them in their tracks with a stern command. 'Come back here!' she called severely. They obeyed with spiritless feet and stood dejectedly before her. 'Go quietly,' ordered Lucia. 'You shouldn't romp when you're on duty. Decimus does not like it.' They looked up shyly from under their long lashes, and Lucia's lips curled into a sympathetic grin that relighted their eyes.

'You may go now,' she said, abruptly resuming a tone of command. Lounging on the long marble seat beside the table, she watched the twins as they marched a few paces behind Decimus, their spines straight and stiff as arrows, accenting each determined step with jerks of their heads from side to side, in a very faithful imitation of the crusty butler. Lucia chuckled. 'The little rascals,' she muttered. 'They deserve to be spanked for that.' Then she suddenly sobered and sat studiously frowning at the rhythmic flexion of her sandalled toes. Marcellus would be here in a moment. How much—if anything—should she tell her adored brother about her unpleasant experience with Gaius? But first, of course, she must discover what dreadful thing had happened last night at the Tribunes' banquet.

*　*　*　*　*　*

'Good morning, sweet child!' Marcellus tipped back his sister's head, noisily kissed her between the eyes, and tousled her hair, while Bambo, his big black sheep-dog, snuggled his grinning muzzle under her arm and wagged amiably.

'Down! Both of you!' commanded Lucia. 'You're uncommonly bright this morning, Tribune Marcellus Lucan Gallio. I thought you were going to a party at the Club.'

'Ah, my infant sister, but what a party!' Marcellus gingerly touched his finely moulded, close-cropped, curly head in several ailing areas, and winced. 'You may well be glad that you are not—and can never be—a Tribune. It was indeed a long, stormy night.'

'A wet one, at any rate, to judge from your puffy eyes. Tell me about it—or as much as you can remember.' Lucia scooped Bambo off the marble lectus with her foot, and her brother seated himself on the seat beside her. He laughed, reminiscently, painfully.

'I fear I disgraced the family. Only the dear gods know what may come of it. His Highness was too far gone to understand, but someone will be sure to tell him before the day is over.'

Lucia leaned forward anxiously, laid a hand on his knee, and searched his cloudy eyes.

'Gaius?' she asked, in a frightened whisper. 'What happened, Marcellus?'

'A poem,' he muttered, 'an ode; a long, tiresome, incredibly stupid ode, wrought for the occasion by old Senator Tuscus, who, having reached that ripeness of senescence where Time and Eternity are mistaken for each other——'

'Sounds as if you'd arrived there, too,' broke in Lucia. 'Can't you speed it up a little?'

'Don't hurry me, impatient youth,' sighed Marcellus. 'I am very frail. As I was saying, this interminable ode, conceived by the ancient Tuscus to improve his repute, was read by his son Antonius, also in need of royal favour; a grandiloquent eulogy to our glorious Prince.'

'He must have loved the flattery,' observed Lucia, 'and of course you all applauded it. You and Tullus, especially.'

'I was just coming to that,' said Marcellus, thickly. 'For hours there had been a succession of rich foods and many beverages; also a plentitude of metal music interspersed with Greek choruses—pretty good—and an exhibition of magic—pretty bad; and some perfunctory speeches, of great length and thickness. A wrestling match, too, I believe. The night was far advanced. Long before Antonius rose, my sister, if any man among us had been free to consult his own desire, we would all have stretched out on our comfortable couches and slept. The gallant Tullus, of whose good health you are ever unaccountably solicitous, sat across from me, frankly asleep like a little child.'

'And then you had the ode,' encouraged Lucia, crisply.

'Yes, we then had the ode. And as Antonius droned on—and on—he seemed to recede farther and farther; his features became dimmer and dimmer; and the measured noise he was making sounded fainter and fainter, as my tortured eyes grew hotter and heavier——'

'Marcellus!' shouted Lucia. 'In the name of every immortal god! Get on with it!'

'Be calm, impetuous child. I do not think rapidly to-day. Never again shall I be anything but dog tired. That ode did something to me, I fear. Well—after it had been creeping along for leagues and decades, I suddenly roused, pulled myself together, and gazed about upon the distinguished company. Almost everyone had peacefully passed away, except a few at the high table whose frozen smiles were held with clenched teeth; and Antonius's insufferable young brother, Quintus, who was purple with anger. I can't stomach that arrogant pup and he knows I despise him.'

'Gaius!' barked Lucia, in her brother's face, so savagely that Bambo growled. 'I want to know what you did to offend Gaius!'

Marcellus laughed whimperingly, for it hurt; then burst into hysterical guffaws.

'If the Glorious One had been merely asleep, quietly, decently, with his fat chins on his bosom—as were his devoted subjects—your unfortunate brother might have borne it. But our Prince had allowed his head to tip far back. His mouth—by no means a thing of beauty, at best—was open. The tongue protruded unprettily and the bulbous nose twitched at each resounding inhalation. Our banquet-hall was deathly quiet, but for Antonius and Gaius, who shared the floor.'

'Revolting!' muttered Lucia.

'A feeble word, my sister. You should give more heed to your diction. Well—at that fateful moment Antonius had reached the climax of his father's ode with an apostrophe to our Prince that must have caused a storm on Mount Parnassus. Gaius was a Fountain of Knowledge! The eyes of Gaius glowed with Divine Light! When the lips of Gaius moved, Wisdom flowed and Justice smiled! . . . Precious child,' went on Marcellus, taking her hand, 'I felt my tragic mishap coming on, not unlike an unbeatable sneeze. I suddenly burst out laughing! No—I do not mean that I chuckled furtively into my hands: I threw back my head and roared! Howled! Long, lusty yells of insane laughter!' Reliving the experience, Marcellus went off again into an abandon of undisciplined mirth. 'Believe me—I woke everybody up—but Gaius.'

'Marcellus!'

Suddenly sobered by the tone of alarm in his sister's voice, he looked into her pale, unsmiling face.

'What is it, Lucia?' he demanded. 'Are you ill?'

'I'm—afraid!' she whispered, weakly.

He put his arms about her and she pressed her forehead against his shoulder.

'There, there!' he murmured. 'We've nothing to fear, Lucia. I was foolish to upset you. I thought you would be amused. Gaius will be angry, of course, when he learns of it; but he will not venture to punish the son of Marcus Lucan Gallio.'

'But—you see——' stammered Lucia, 'it was only yesterday that Father openly criticized him in the Senate. Had you not heard?'

'Of course; but the Pater's strong enough to take care of himself,' declared Marcellus, almost too confidently to be convincing. There was a considerable pause before his sister spoke. He felt her trembling.

'If it were just that one thing,' she said, slowly, 'perhaps it might be overlooked. But—now you have offended him. And he was already angry with me.'

'You!' Marcellus took her by the shoulders and stared into her worried eyes. 'And why should Gaius be angry with you?'

'Do you remember, last summer, when Diana and her mother and I were guests at the Palace on Capri—and Gaius came to visit the Emperor?'

'Well? Go on!' demanded Marcellus. 'What of it? What did he say? What did he do?'

'He tried to make love to me.'

'That loathsome beast!' roared Marcellus, leaping to his feet. 'I'll tear his dirty tongue out! I'll gouge his eyes out with my thumbs! Why haven't you told me this before?'

'You have given the reason,' said Lucia, dejectedly. 'I was afraid of the tongue-tearing—and eye-gouging. Had my brother been a puny, timid man, I might have told him at once. But my brother is strong and brave—and reckless. Now that I have told him, he will kill Gaius; and my brother, whom I so dearly love, will be put to death, and my father, too, I suppose. And my mother will be banished or imprisoned and——'

'What did Mother think about this?' broke in Marcellus.

'I did not tell her.'

'Why not? You should have done so—instantly!'

'Then she would have told Father. That would have been as dangerous as telling my brother.'

'You should have told the Emperor!' spluttered Marcellus. 'Tiberius is no monument to virtue, but he would have done something about that! He's not so very fond of Gaius.'

'Don't be foolish! That half-crazy old man? He would probably have gone into one of his towering tantrums, and scolded Gaius in the presence of everybody; and then he would have cooled off and forgotten all about it. But Gaius wouldn't have forgotten! No—I decided to ignore it. Nobody knows—but Diana.'

'Diana! If you thought you had such a dangerous secret, why should you tell that romping infant Diana?'

'Because she was afraid of him, too, and understood my reasons for not wanting to be left alone with him. But Diana is not a baby, Marcellus. She is nearly sixteen. And—if you'll pardon my saying so—I think you should stop mussing her hair, and tickling her under the chin, when she comes here to visit me—as if she were five, and you a hundred.'

'Sorry! It hadn't occurred to me that she would resent my playful caresses. I never thought of her except as a child—like yourself.'

'Well—it's time you realized that Diana is a young woman. If she resents your playful caresses, it is not because they are caresses but because they are playful.' Lucia hesitated; then continued softly, her eyes intent on her brother's gloomy face. 'She might even like your caresses—if they meant anything. I think it hurts her, Marcellus, when you call her "Sweetheart." '

'I had not realized that Diana was so sensitive,' mumbled Marcellus. 'She is certainly stormy enough when anything displeases her. She was audacious enough to demand that her name be changed.'

'She hated to be called Asinia, Marcellus,' said Lucia, loyally. 'Diana is prettier, don't you think?'

'Perhaps,' shrugged Marcellus. 'Name of a silly goddess. The name of the Asinius stock is noble; means something!'

'Don't be tiresome, Marcellus!' snapped Lucia. 'What I am saying is: Diana would probably enjoy having you call her "Sweetheart" if——'

Marcellus, who had been restlessly panthering about, drew up to inspect his sister with sudden interest.

'Are you trying to imply that this youngster thinks she is fond of me?'

'Of course! And I think you're pretty dense, not to have noticed it! Come and sit down—and compose yourself. Our breakfast is on the way.'

Marcellus glanced casually in the direction of the house; then stared frowningly; then rubbed his eyes with his fists, and stared again. Lucia's lips puckered into a reluctant grin.

'In truth, my sister,' he groaned, 'I am in much worse condition than I had supposed.'

'You're all right, Tribune,' she drawled. 'There really are two of them.'

'Thanks! I am relieved. Are they as bright as they are beautiful?' he asked, as the twins approached.

'It is too early to tell. This is their first day on duty. Don't frighten them, Marcellus. They're already scared half out of their wits. They have never worked before . . . No, no, Bambo! Come here!'

Rosy with embarrassment, the Macedonians began unburdening their silver trays, fussily pretending they were not under observation.

'Quaint little things; aren't they?' chirped Marcellus. 'Where did Father pick them up?'

'Don't!' whispered Lucia. She rose and walked to the balustrade, her brother sauntering after her. They turned their faces toward the city. 'What did Tullus think of what you did?' she asked, irrelevantly.

'Tell me'—Marcellus ignored her query—'is there anything peculiar about these slaves that makes you so extraordinarily considerate?' Lucia shook her head, without looking up, and sighed.

'I was just thinking,' she said, at length, 'how I might feel if I were in their place.' Her troubled eyes lifted to meet his look of inquiry.

'It is not impossible, Marcellus, that I may soon find myself in some such predicament. . . . You wouldn't like that. Would you?'

'Nonsense!' he growled, out of the corner of his mouth. 'You're making too great a disaster of this! Nothing's going to happen. I'll see to that.'

'How?' demanded Lucia. 'How are you going to see to it?'

'Well,' temporized Marcellus, 'what do you think I should do—short of going to that ugly reptile with an apology?'

Lucia brightened a little and laid her hand on his arm.

'Do that!' she pleaded. 'To-day! Make peace with him, Marcellus! Tell him you were drunk. You were; weren't you?'

'I'd rather be flogged—in the market-place!'

'Yes, I know. And perhaps you will be. Gaius is dangerous!'

'Ah, what could he do ? Tiberius would not permit his half-witted stepson to punish a member of the Gallio family. It's common knowledge that the old man despises him.'

'Yes, but Tiberius consented to his regency because Julia demanded it. And Julia still has to be reckoned with. If it came to a decision whether that worn-out old man should stand up for the Gallio family —against Gaius—with his shrewish wife screaming in his ears, I doubt that he would trouble himself. Julia would stop at nothing!'

'The vindictive old——' Marcellus paused on the edge of a kennel word.

'Think it over.' Lucia's tone was brighter, as if she felt herself gaining ground. 'Come—let us eat our breakfast. Then you will go to Gaius, and take your medicine. Praise him! Flatter him! He can stand any amount of it. Tell him he is beautiful! Tell him there's nobody in the whole Empire as wise as he is. Tell him he is divine! But—be sure you keep your face straight. Gaius already knows you have a keen sense of humour.'

* * * * * *

Having decided to accept his sister's counsel, Marcellus was anxious to perform his unpleasant duty and be done with it. Prudence suggested that he seek an interview through the formal channels and await the convenience of the Prince; but, increasingly impressed by the gravity of his position, he resolved to ignore the customary court procedure and take a chance of seeing Gaius without an appointment. By appearing at the Palace shortly before noon, he might even be lucky enough to have a few minutes alone with the Prince before anyone had informed him about last night's mishap.

At ten, rejuvenated by a hot bath, a vigorous massage by Demetrius, and a plunge in the pool, the Tribune returned to his rooms, dressed with care, and sauntered downstairs. Observing that the library door was ajar, he paused to greet his father, whom he had not seen since yesterday. The handsome, white-haired Senator was seated at his desk, writing. He glanced up, nodded, smiled briefly, and invited Marcellus to come in.

'If you are at liberty to-day, my son, I should be pleased to have you go with me to inspect a span of matched Hispanian mares.'

'I should like to, sir; but might to-morrow serve as well? I have an important errand to do; something that cannot be put off.' There was a note of anxiety in the Tribune's voice that narrowed the wise old eyes.

'Nothing serious, I trust.' Gallio pointed to a vacant seat.

'I hope not, sir.' Marcellus sat tentatively on the broad arm of the chair as a fair compromise between candid reticence and complete explanation.

'Your manner,' observed his father, pointedly, 'suggests that you are worried. I have no wish to intrude upon your private perplexities, but is there anything I might do for you?'

'I'm afraid not, sir; thank you.' After a moment of indecision, Marcellus slowly slid into the chair and regarded his distinguished parent with a sober face. 'If you have the time, I will tell you.'

Gallio nodded, put down his stylus, and leaned forward on his folded arms encouragingly. It was quite a long narrative. Marcellus did not spare himself. He told it all. At one juncture he was half-disposed to introduce Lucia's dilemma as relevant to his own; but decided against it, feeling that their parent was getting about all he could stand for one session. He concluded, at length, with the declaration that he was going at once to apologize. Gallio, who had listened attentively but without comment, now shook his leonine head and shouted 'No!' He straightened and shook his head again. 'No!—No, no!'

Amazed by his father's outburst, for he had anticipated his full approval, Marcellus asked, 'Why not, sir?'

'The most dangerous implement a man can use for the repair of a damaged relationship is an abject apology.' Gallio pushed back his huge chair and rose to his full height as if preparing to deliver an address. 'Even in the most favourable circumstances, as when placating an injured friend, a self-abasing apology may do much harm. If the friend is contented with nothing less, he should not be served with it at all; for his friendship is not worth its upkeep. In the case of Gaius, an apology would be fatal; for you are not dealing here with a gentleman, but with a congenital scoundrel. Your apology will imply that you expect Gaius to be generous. Generosity, in his opinion, is a sign of weakness. By imputing it to him, you will have given him further offence. Gaius has reasons to be sensitive about his power. Never put yourself on the defensive with a man who is fretting about his own insecurity. Here, he says, is at least one opportunity to demonstrate my strength.'

'Perhaps you are right, sir,' conceded Marcellus.

'Perhaps? Of course, I am right!' The Senator walked to the door, closed it softly, and resumed his seat. 'And that is not all,' he went on. 'Let me refresh your mind about the peculiar relations in the imperial family which explain why Gaius is a man to be watched and feared. There is old Tiberius, alternately raging and rotting in his fifty-room villa on Capri; a pathetic and disgusting figure, mooning over his necromancies and chattering to his gods—My son,' Gallio interrupted himself, 'there is always something fundamentally wrong with a rich man or a king who pretends to be religious. Let the poor and helpless invoke the gods. That is what the gods are for—to distract the attention of the weak from their otherwise intolerable miseries. When an emperor makes much ado about religion, he is either cracked or crooked. Tiberius is not crooked. If he is cracked, the cause is not far to seek. For a score of years he has nursed a bitter grudge against his mother for demanding that he divorce Vipsania—the only creature he ever loved——'

'I think he is fond of Diana,' interjected Marcellus.

'True! And why? He is fond of the child because she is Vipsania's granddaughter. Let us remember that he was not a bad ruler in his earlier days. Rome had never known such prosperity; not even under Julius. As you know, when Vipsania passed out of his life, Tiberius went to pieces; lost all interest in the Empire; surrounded himself with soothsayers, mountebanks, priests, and astrologers. Presently his mind was so deranged by all this nonsense that he consented to marry Julia, whom he had despised from childhood.' The Senator chuckled, not very pleasantly, and remarked: 'Perhaps that was why he wished to be relieved of all his administrative duties. He found that to hate Julia as adequately as she deserved to be hated, he had to make it a full-time occupation. So—there was the vixenish Julia, together with the obnoxious offspring she had whelped before he married her. And he has not only hated Julia: he has been deathly afraid of her—and with good reason, for she has the morbid mind of an assassin—and the courage, too.'

'Lucia says the old gentleman never touches his wine, at table, until the Empress has tasted it,' put in Marcellus, 'but she thought that was just a little family joke.'

'We will not disturb your young sister with any other interpretation,' advised the Senator, 'but it is no joke; nor is Tiberius merely trying to be playful when he stations a dozen Numidian gladiators at the doors and windows of his bed-chamber. . . . Now, these facts are, I suspect, never absent very long from Gaius's mind. He knows that the Emperor is half-insane ; that his mother lives precariously; and that if anything should happen to her his regency would last no longer than it takes a galley to clear for Crete with a deposed prince on board.'

'Were that to happen,' broke in Marcellus, 'who would succeed Gaius?'

'Well——' Gallio slighted the query with a shrug. 'It will not happen. If anyone dies, down there, it won't be Julia. You can depend on that.'

'But, just supposing '—persisted Marcellus. ' If, for any reason—accident, illness, or forthright murder—Julia should be eliminated—and Gaius, too, in consequence—do you think Tiberius might put Asinius Gallus on the throne?'

'It is possible,' said Gallio. 'The Emperor might feel that he was making tardy amends to Vipsania by honouring her son. And Gallus would be no mean choice. No Roman has ever commanded more respect than Pollio, his learned sire. Gallus would have the full support of our legions—both at home and abroad. However,' he added, half to himself, 'a brave soldier does not inevitably make a wise monarch. Your military commander has only a foreign foe to fight. All that he requires is tactics and bravery. An emperor is forever at war with a jealous court, an obstreperous Senate, and a swarm of avaricious land-holders. What he needs is a keen scent for conspiracy, a mind crafty enough to outmanoeuvre treachery, a natural talent for duplicity—and the hide of an alligator.'

'Thick enough to turn the point of a stiletto,' assisted Marcellus.

'It is a hazardous occupation,' nodded Gallio, 'but I do not think our excellent friend Gallus will ever be exposed to its dangers.'

'I wonder how Diana would like being a princess,' remarked Marcellus, absently. He glanced up to find his father's eyes alight with curiosity.

'We are quite far afield, aren't we ; discussing Diana ?' observed Gallio, slyly. ' Are you interested in her?'

'Not any more than Lucia is,' replied Marcellus, elaborately casual. 'They are, as you know, inseparable. Naturally, I see Diana almost every day.'

'A beautiful and amazingly vivacious child,' commented the Senator.

'Beautiful and vivacious,' agreed Marcellus, 'but not a child. Diana is nearly sixteen, you know.'

'Old enough to be married, is that what you are trying to say ? You could hardly do better—if she can be tamed. Diana has fine blood. Sixteen, eh ? It is a wonder Gaius has not noticed. He might do himself much good in the esteem of the Emperor—and he certainly is in need of it—if he should win Diana's favour.'

'She loathes him!'

'Indeed? Then she has talked with you about it?'

'No, sir. Lucia told me.'

There was a considerable interval of silence before Gallio spoke again, slowly measuring his words.

'In your present strained relations with Gaius, my son, you would show discretion, I think, if you made your attentions to Diana as inconspicuous as possible.'

'I never see her anywhere else than here, sir.'

'Even so: treat her casually. Gaius has spies everywhere.'

'Here—in our house?' Marcellus frowned incredulously.

'Why not ? Do you think that Gaius, the son of Agrippa, who never had an honest thought in his life, and of Julia, who was born with both ears shaped like keyholes, would be too honourable for that?' Gallio deftly rolled up the scroll that lay at his elbow, indicating that he was ready to put aside his work for the day. 'We have discussed this fully enough, I think. As for what occurred last night, the Prince's friends may advise him to let the matter drop. Your best course is to do nothing, say nothing—and wait developments.' He rose and straightened the lines of his toga. 'Come! Let us ride to Ismael's camp and look at the Hispanians. You will like them; milk-white, high-spirited, intelligent—and undoubtedly expensive. Ismael, the old rascal, knows I am interested in them, unfortunately for my purse.'

Marcellus responded eagerly to his father's elevated mood. It was almost as if the shrewd Marcus Lucan Gallio had firmly settled the unhappy affair with Gaius. He opened the door for the Senator to precede him. In the atrium, leaning against a column, lounged Demetrius. Coming smartly to attention he saluted with his spear and followed a few paces behind the two men as they strolled through the vasty rooms and out to the spacious western portico.

'Rather unusual for Demetrius to be loitering in the atrium,' remarked Marcellus in a guarded undertone.

'Perhaps he was standing there,' surmised Gallio, 'to discourage anyone else from loitering by the door.'

'Do you think he may have had a special reason for taking that precaution?'

'Possibly. He was with you at the banquet; knows that you gave offence to Gaius; concludes that you are in disfavour; and, by adding it all up, thinks it is time to be viligant.'

'Shall I ask him if he suspects that there are spies in the house?' suggested Marcellus.

Gallio shook his head.

'If he observes anything irregular, he will tell you, my son.'

'I wonder who this is coming.' Marcellus nodded toward a uniformed Equestrian Knight who had just turned in from the Via Aurelia. 'We're to be honoured,' he growled. 'It is Quintus, the younger Tuscus. The Prince has been seing much of him lately, I hear.'

The youthful Tribune, followed by a well-mounted aide, rode briskly toward them; and, neglecting to salute, drew a gilded scroll from the belt of his tunic.

'I am ordered by His Highness, Prince Gaius, to deliver this message into the hands of Tribune Marcellus Lucan Gallio,' he barked, haughtily. The aide, who had dismounted, carried the scroll up the steps and handed it over.

'His Highness might do well to employ messengers with better manners,' drawled Marcellus. 'Are you to await an answer?'

'Imperial commands require obedience, not replies!' shouted Quintus. He pulled his horse about savagely, dug in his spurs, and made off, pursued by his obsequious aide.

'Gaius is prompt,' commented the Senator. There was satisfaction on his face as he watched his son's steady hands, and the cool deliberateness with which he drew his dagger and thrust the point of it through the wax. Unrolling the ostentatious document, Marcellus held it at an angle where his father might share its contents. Gallio read it aloud, in a rasping undertone:

Prince Gaius Drusus Agrippa to Trib. Marcellus Lucan Gallio:
    Greeting:
        The courage of a Military Tribune should not be squandered in banquet-halls. It should be serving the Empire in positions where reckless audacity is honourable and valorous. Tribune Marcellus Lucan Gallio is commanded to report, before sunset, at the Praetorium of Chief Legate M. Cornelius Capito, and receive his commission.

Marcellus rolled up the scroll, tossed it negligently to Demetrius, who thrust it into the breast of his tunic; and, turning to his father, remarked, 'We have plenty of time to go out and see Ismael's horses.'

The Senator proudly drew himself erect, gave his son a respectful bow, strutted down the marble steps; and, taking the bridle reins, mounted his mettlesome black gelding. Marcellus beckoned to Demetrius.

'You heard that message?' he queried, abruptly.

'Not if it was private, sir,' countered Demetrius.

'Sounds a bit malicious,' observed Marcellus. 'The Prince evidently wishes to dispose of me.'

'Yes, sir,' agreed Demetrius.

'Well—I brought this upon myself,' said Marcellus. 'I shall not order you to risk your life. You are at liberty to decide whether——'

'I shall go with you, sir.'

'Very good. Inspect my equipment—and look over your own tackle, too.' Marcellus started down the steps, and turned to say, soberly, 'You're going to your death, you know.'

'Yes, sir,' said Demetrius. 'You will need some heavier sandals, sir. Shall I get them?'

'Yes—and several pairs for yourself. Ask Marcipor for the money.'

After a lively tussle with the bay, who was impatient to overtake her stable-mate, Marcellus drew up beside the Senator, and they slowed their horses to a trot.

'I tarried for a word with Demetrius. I shall take him with me.'

'Of course.'

'I told him he might decide.'

'That was quite proper.'

'I told him he might never come back alive.'

'Probably not,' said the Senator, grimly, 'but you can be assured that he will never come back alone.'

'Demetrius is a very sound fellow—for a slave,' observed Marcellus.

The Senator made no immediate rejoinder, but his stern face and flexed jaw indicated that his reflections were weighty.

'My son,' he said, at length, staring moodily down the road, 'we could do with a few men in the Roman Senate with the brains and bravery of your slave Demetrius.' He pulled his horse down to a walk. ' "Demetrius is a sound fellow—for a slave", eh? Well—his being a slave does not mean that what he thinks, what he says, and what he does are unimportant. One of these days the slaves are going to take over this rotted Government! They could do it to-morrow if they were organized. You might say that their common desire for liberty should unite them, but that is not enough. All men want more liberty than they have. What the Roman slaves lack is leadership. In time, that will come. You shall see!' The senator paused so long, after this amazing declaration, that Marcellus felt some response was in order. 'I never heard you express that opinion before, sir. Do you think there will be an uprising—among the slaves?' 'It lacks form,' replied Gallio. 'It lacks cohesion. But some day it will take shape; it will be integrated; it will develop a leader, a cause, a slogan, a banner. Three-fourths of this city's inhabitants either have been or are slaves. Daily our expeditionary forces arrive with new shiploads of them. It would require a very shrewd and powerful Government to keep in subjugation a force three times its size and strength. But—look at our Government! A mere hollow shell! It has no moral fibre! Content with its luxury, indolence, and profligacy, its extravagant pageants in honour of its silly gods; ruled by an insane dotard and a drunken nonentity! no, my son, Rome is doomed! I do not venture to predict when or how Nemesis will arrive—but it is on its way. The Roman Empire is too weak and wicked to survive!'

Chapter II

CORNELIUS CAPITO was not at home when Marcellus called at three to learn what Gaius had planned for him. This was surprising and rather ominous too. The conspicuous absence of the Chief Legate, and his deputizing of a young understrapper to handle the case, clearly meant that Capito had no relish for an unpleasant interview with the son of his lifelong friend.

The Gallios had walked their horses for the last two miles of the journey in from Ismael's camp, where the Senator had declined to purchase the Hispanian mares at the exorbitant price demanded by the avaricious old Syrian, though it was plain to see that the day's events had dulled his interest in the negotiation.

The Senator's mind was fully occupied now with speculations about Cornelius. If anybody in Rome could temper the punitive undertaking which Gaius intended for his son, it would be the Commander of the Praetorian Guard and Chief of the Legates who wielded an enormous power in the making of appointments.

Slipping into a reminiscent—and candidly pessimistic—mood, the elder Gallio had recited the deplorable story they both knew by heart, the dismal epic of the Praetorian Guard. Marcellus had been brought up on it. As if his son had never heard the tale before, the Senator began far back in the time when Julius Caesar had created this organi-

zation for his own security.   Picked men they were, with notable records
for daring deeds. As the years rolled on, the traditions of the Praetorian
Guard became richer.   A magnificent armoury was built to house its
battle trophies, and in its spacious atrium were erected bronze and
marble tablets certifying to the memorable careers of its heroes.   To
be a member of the Praetorian Guard in those great—long since out-
moded—days when courage and integrity were valuable property, was
the highest honour the Empire could bestow.

Then, Gallio had continued gloomily, Augustus—whose vanity had
swollen into a monstrous, stinking, cancerous growth—had begun to
confer honorary memberships upon his favourites; upon Senators who
slavishly approved his mistakes and weren't above softening the royal
sandal-straps with their saliva; upon certain rich men who had fattened
on manipulations in foreign loot; upon wealthy slave-brokers, dealers
in stolen sculpture; upon provincial revenue-collectors; upon almost
anybody indeed who could minister to the diseased Augustan ego or
pour ointment on his itching avarice.   And thus had passed away the
glory and distinction of the Praetorian Guard.   Its memberships were
for sale.

For a little while, Tiberius had tried to arrest its accelerating descent
into hell.   Cornelius Capito, who had so often led a legion into suicidal
forays that a legend had taken shape about him—for were not the gods
directing a man whose life was so cheaply held and so miraculously
preserved?—was summoned home to be Commander of the Praetorian
Guard.   Capito had not wanted the office, but had obeyed the command.
With the same kind of recklessness that had won him honours on many
a battlefield, he had begun to clean up the discredited institution.   But
it hadn't been long before hard pressure on Tiberius made it necessary
for the Emperor to caution the uncompromising warrior about his
honest zeal.   He mustn't go too far in this business of cleansing the
Praetorian Guard.

'It was then,' declaimed Gallio, 'that brave old Capito discovered,
to his dismay, why Tiberius had called him to be the Commander;
simply to use his name as a deodorant!'

Marcellus had realized, at this juncture of his father's painful reflections, that the remainder of the story would be somewhat embarrass-
ing; for it concerned the Military Tribunes.

'If Augustus had only been content,' the Senator was proceeding
according to plan, 'with his destruction of the Praetorian Guard!   Perhaps, had he foreseen the result of his policy there, not even his rapaci-
ous greed could have induced him to work the same havoc with the
Order of Tribunes.   But you know what happened, my son.'

Yes, Marcellus knew. The Order of Tribunes had been honourable too. You had to be a Tribune, in deed and in truth, if you wanted to wear its insignia. Like the Praetorian Guard, it too was handsomely quartered. Tribunes, home on furlough or recovering from injuries or awaiting orders, took advantage of the library, the baths, the commissary that the Empire had provided for them. Then Augustus had decided to expand the Order of Tribunes to include all sons of Senators and influential taxpayers. You needn't ever have shouted an order or spent a night in a tent. If your father had enough money and political weight, you could wear the uniform and receive the salute.

Marcellus liked to think that his own case was not quite so indefensible as most of them. He had not been a mere playboy. At the Academy he had given his full devotion to the history of military campaigns, strategy, and tactics. He was an accomplished athlete, expert with the javelin, a winner of many prizes for marksmanship with the bow. He handled a duelling sword with the skill of a professional gladiator.

Nor had his recreations been profitless. Aristocratic youths, eligible to the hierarchy of public offices, disdained any actual practice of the fine arts. They affected to be critics and connoisseurs of painting and sculpture, but would have experienced much embarrassment had they been caught with a brush or chisel in hand. Independent of this taboo, Marcellus had taken a serious interest in sculpture, much to the delight of his father, who—upon observing that he had a natural genius for it—had provided him with competent tutors.

But—sometimes he had been appropriately sensitive about his status as a Military Tribune when, as happened infrequently, some *real* Tribune arrived at the ornate clubhouse, bronzed and battered and bandaged, after gruelling months on active duty.

However, Marcellus said to himself, it wasn't as if he had no qualifications for military service. He was abundantly prepared to accept a commission if required to do so. Occasionally he had wished that an opportunity for such service might arise. He had never been asked to take a command. And a man would be a fool, indeed, to seek a commission. War was a swinish business, intended for bullies who liked to strut their medals and yell obscenities at their inferiors and go for weeks without a bath. He could do all this if he had to. He didn't have to; but he had never been honestly proud of his title. Sometimes when Decimus addressed him as 'Tribune'—which was the surly fellow's custom on such occasions as serving him his late breakfast in bed—Marcellus was tempted to slap him, and would have done so had he a better case.

They had ridden in silence for a little time, after the Senator had aired his favourite grievances.

'Once in a while,' continued Gallio, meditatively, 'crusty Capito—like blind Samson of the Hebrew myth—rouses to have his way. I am hopeful that he may intervene in your behalf, my son. If it is an honourable post, we will not lament even though it involves peril. I am prepared to hand you over to danger—but not to disgrace. I cannot believe that my trusted friend will fail to do his utmost for you, to-day. I bid you to approach him with that expectation!'

His father had seemed so confident of this outcome that the remainder of their ride had been almost enjoyable. Assured that the gruff but loyal old warrior, who had helped him into his first white toga, would see to it that no indignities were practised on him by a petulant and vengeful Prince, Marcellus set off light-heartedly to the impressive headquarters of the Chief Legate.

Accompanied by Demetrius, who was himself a striking figure in the saddle, he rode through the increasingly crowded streets on the way to the huge circular plaza, around half of which were grouped the impressive marble buildings serving the Praetorian Guard and ranking officials of the army. To the left stretched a vast parade-ground, now entirely filled with loaded camel caravans and hundreds of pack-asses.

An expedition was mobilizing, ready for departure on the long trip to Gaul. The plaza was a stirring scene. Banners fluttered. The young officers were smart in their field uniforms. The legionaries were alert, spirited, apparently eager to be on their way. Maybe an experience of this sort would be stimulating, thought Marcellus.

Unable to ride into the plaza, because of the congestion, they dismounted in the street, Marcellus handing his reins to Demetrius, and proceeding through the narrow lane toward the Praetorium. The broad corridors were filled with Centurions awaiting orders. Many of them he knew. They smiled recognition and saluted. Perhaps they surmised that he was here on some such business as their own, and it gave him a little thrill of pride. You could think what you liked about the brutishness and griminess of war, it was no small honour to be a Roman soldier—whatever your rank! He shouldered his way to the open door leading into Capito's offices.

'The Commander is not in,' rasped the busy deputy. 'He ordered me to deliver this commission to you.'

Marcellus took the heavily sealed scroll from the fellow's hand, hesitated a moment, half-inclined to inquire whether Capito expected to return presently, decided against it; turned, and went out, down the broad steps and across the densely packed plaza. Demetrius, seeing

him coming, led the horses forward and handed his master the bay
mare's bridle-reins. Their eyes met. After all, thought Marcellus,
Demetrius had a right to know where we stood in this business.

'I have not opened it yet,' he said, tapping the scroll. 'Let us go
home.'

*   *   *   *   *   *

The Senator was waiting for him in the library.

'Well, what did our friend Capito have for you?' he asked, making
no attempt to disguise his uneasiness.

'He was not there. A deputy served me.' Marcellus laid the scroll
on the desk and sat down to wait while his father impatiently thrust
his knife through the heavy seals. For what seemed a very long time
the narrowed eyes raced the length of the pompous manifesto. Then
Gallio cleared his throat, and faced his son with troubled eyes.

'You are ordered to take command of the garrison at Minoa,' he
muttered.

'Where's Minoa?'

'Minoa is a villainously dirty little port city in southern Palestine.'

'I never heard of it,' said Marcellus. 'I know about our forts at
Caesarea and Joppa; but—what have we at this Minoa?'

'It is the point of departure for the old trail that leads to the Dead
Sea. Most of our salt comes from there, as you probably know. The
duty of our garrison at Minoa is to make that road safe for our caravans.'

'Doesn't sound like a very interesting job,' commented Marcellus.
'I was anticipating something dangerous.'

'Well, you will not be disappointed. It is dangerous enough. The
Bedouins who menace that salt trail are notoriously brutal savages.
But because they are independent gangs of bandits, with refuges in
that rocky desert region, we have never undertaken a campaign to
crush them. It would have required five legions.' The Senator was
speaking as if he were very well informed about Minoa, and Marcellus
was listening with full attention.

'You mean these desert brigands steal the salt from our caravans?'

'No, not the salt. They plunder the caravans on the way in, for
they have to carry supplies and money to hire labourers at the salt
deposits. Many of the caravans that set out over that trail are never
heard from again. But that isn't quite all,' the Senator continued.
'We have not been wasting very good men in the fort at Minoa. The
garrison is composed of a tough lot of rascals. More than half of them
were once commissioned officers who, for rank insubordination or other
irregularities, are in disfavour with the Government. The lesser half is

made up of an assortment of brawlers whose politics bred discontent.'
'I thought the Empire had a more prompt and less expensive method
of dealing with objectionable people.'
'There are some cases,' explained the Senator, 'in which a public
trial or a private assassination might stir up a protest. In these
instances, it is as effective—and more practical—to send the offender
to Minoa.'
'Why, sir, this is equivalent to exile!' Marcellus rose, bent forward
over his father's desk, and leaned his weight on his white-knuckled
fists. 'Do you know anything more about this dreadful place?'
Gallio slowly nodded his head.
'I know all about it, my son. For many years, one of my special
duties in the Senate—together with four of my colleagues—has been
the supervision of that fort.' He paused, and began slowly rising to
his feet, his deep-lined face livid with anger. 'I believe that was why
Gaius Drusus Agrippa——' The Senator savage· ground the hatred
name to bits with his teeth. 'He planned this for \ · son—because he
knew—that I would know—what you were going \ ɔ.' Raising his
arms high, and shaking his fists in rage, Gallio shoute 'Now I would
that I were religious! I would beseech some god to d. in his soul!'

*   *   *   *   *   *

Cornelia Vipsania Gallio, who always slightly accented her middle
name—though she was only a stepdaughter to the divorced spouse of
Emperor Tiberius—might have been socially important had he made
the necessary effort.
If mere wishing on Cornelia's part could have induced her h sband
to ingratiate himself with the Crown, Marcus Lucan Gallio could have
belonged to the inner circle, and any favour he desired for himself or
his family might have been granted; or if Cornelia herself had gone to
the trouble of fawning upon the insufferable old Julia, the Gallio household might have reached that happy elevation by this shorter route.
But Cornelia lacked the necessary energy.
She was an exquisite creature, even in her middle forties; a person
of considerable culture, a gracious hostess, an affectionate wife, an
indulgent mother, and probably the laziest woman in the whole Roman
Empire. It was said that sometimes slaves would serve the Gallio
establishment for months before discovering that their mistress was
not an invalid.
Cornelia had her breakfast in bed at noon, lounged in her rooms or
in the sunny garden all the afternoon, drowsed over the classics,
apathetically swept her slim fingers across the strings of her pandura;

and was waited on, hand and foot, by everybody in the house. And everybody loved her, too, for she was kind and easy to please. Moreover, she never gave orders—except for her personal comfort. The slaves—under the competent and loyal supervision of Marcipor, and the diligent, if somewhat surly, dictatorship of Decimus in the culinary department—managed the institution unaided by her counsel and untroubled by her criticism. She was by nature an optimist, possibly because fretting was laborious. On rare occasions, she was briefly baffled by unhappy events, and at such times she wept quietly—and recovered.

Yesterday, however, something had seriously disturbed her habitual tranquillity. The Senator had made a speech. Paula Gallus, calling in the late afternoon, had told her. Paula had been considerably upset.

Cornelia was not surprised by the report that her famous husband was pessimistic in regard to the current administration of the Roman government, for he was accustomed to walking the floor of her bed-chamber while delivering opinions of this nature; but she was shocked to learn that Marcus had given the Senate the full benefit of his accumulated dissatisfactions. Cornelia had no need to ask Paula why she was so concerned. Paula didn't want Senator Gallio to get himself into trouble with the Crown. In the first place, it would be awkward for Diana to continue her close friendship with Lucia if the latter's eminent parent persisted in baiting Prince Gaius. And, too, was there not a long-standing conspiracy between Paula and Cornelia to encourage an alliance of their houses whenever Diana and Marcellus should become romantically aware of each other?

Paula had not hinted at these considerations when informing Cornelia that the Senator was cutting an impressive figure on some pretty thin ice, but she had gone so far as to remind her long-time friend that Prince Gaius—while notably unskilful at everything else—was amazingly resourceful and ingenious when it came to devising reprisals for his critics.

'But what can I do about it?' Cornelia had moaned languidly. 'Surely you're not hoping that I will rebuke him? My husband would not like to have people telling him what he may say in the Senate.'

'Not even his wife?' Paula arched her patrician brows.

'Especially his wife,' rejoined Cornelia. 'We have a tacit understanding that Marcus is to attend to his profession without my assistance. My responsibility is to manage his home.'

Paula had grinned dryly; and, shortly after, had taken her departure, leaving behind her a distressing dilemma. Cornelia wished that the Senator could be a little less candid. He was such an amiable man when he wanted to be. Of course, Gaius was a waster and a fool; but, after all, he was the Prince Regent, and it wasn't judicious to call him names in public assemblies. First thing you knew, they'd all be black-listed. Paula Gallus was far too prudent to let Diana become involved in their scrapes. If the situation became serious, they wouldn't be seeing much more of Diana. That would be a great grief to Lucia. And it might affect the future of Marcellus, too. It was precious little attention he had paid to the high-spirited young Diana, but Cornelia was still hopeful.

Sometimes she worried, for a moment or two, about Marcellus. One of her most enjoyable dreams posed her son on a beautiful white horse, leading a victorious army through the streets, acknowledging with dignity the plaudits of a multitude no man could number. To be sure, you didn't head that sort of parade unless you had risked some perils; but Marcellus had never been a coward. All he needed was a chance to show what kind of stuff he was made of. He would probably never get that chance now. Cornelia cried bitterly; and because there was no one else to talk to about it, she bared her heart to Lucia. And Lucia, shocked at her mother's unprecedented display of emotion, had tried to console her.

But to-day Cornelia had quite disposed of her anxiety; not because the reason for it had been in any way relieved, but because she was temperamentally incapable of concentrating diligently upon anything—not even upon a threatened catastrophe.

*　　*　　*　　*　　*　　*

About four o'clock (Cornelia was in her luxurious sitting-room, gently combing her shaggy terrier) the Senator entered and without speaking dropped wearily into chair, frowning darkly.

'Tired?' asked Cornelia, tenderly. 'Of course you are. That long ride. And you were disappointed with the Hispanian horses, I think. What was the matter with them?'

'Marcellus has been ordered into service,' growled Gallio, abruptly.

Cornelia pushed the dog off her lap and leaned forward interestedly.

'But this is as it should be, don't you think? We had expected that it might happen some day. Perhaps we should be glad. Will it take him far away?'

'Yes.' The Senator nodded impressively. 'Far away. He has been ordered to command the fort at Minoa.'

'Command! How very nice for him! Minoa! Our son is to be the commander—of the Roman fort—at Minoa! We shall be proud!'

'No!' Gallio shook his white head. 'No! We shall not be proud!

Minoa, my dear, is where we send men to be well rid of them. They have little to do there but quarrel. They are a mob of mutinous cut-throats. We frequently have to appoint a new commander.' He paused for a long, moody moment. 'This time the Senate Committee on affairs at Minoa was not consulted about the appointment. Our son had his orders directly from Gaius.'

This was too much even for the well-balanced Cornelia. She broke into a storm of weeping; noisily hysterical weeping; her fingers digging frantically into the glossy black hair that had tumbled about her shapely shoulders; moaning painful and incoherent reproaches that gradually became intelligible. Racked with sobs, Cornelia amazed them both by crying out, 'Why did you do it, Marcus? Oh, why did you have to bring this tragedy upon our son? Was it so important that you should denounce Gaius—at such a cost to Marcellus—and all of us? Oh, I wish I could have died before this day!'

Gallio bowed his head in his hands and made no effort to share the blame with Marcellus. His son was in plenty of trouble without the added burden of a rebuke from his overwrought mother.

'Where is he?' she asked, thickly, trying to compose herself. 'I must see him.'

'Packing his kit, I think,' muttered Gallio. 'He is ordered to leave at once. A galley will take him to Ostia where a ship sails to-morrow.'

'A ship? What ship? If he must go, why cannot he travel in a manner consistent with his rank? Surely he can charter or buy a vessel, and sail in comfort as becomes a Tribune.'

'There is no time for that, my dear. They are leaving to-night.'

'They? Marcellus—and who else?'

'Demetrius.'

'Well, the gods be thanked for that much!' Cornelia broke out again into tempestuous weeping. 'Why doesn't Marcellus come to see me?' she sobbed.

'He will, in a little while,' said Gallio. 'He wanted me to tell you about it first. And I hope you will meet him in the spirit of a courageous Roman matron.' The Senator's tone was almost severe now. 'Our son has received some very unhappy tidings. He is bearing them manfully calmly, according to our best traditions. But I do not think he could bear to see his mother destroy herself in his presence.'

'Destroy myself!' Cornelia, stunned by the words, faced him with anguished eyes. 'You know I could never do such a thing as that—no matter what happened to us!'

'One does not have to swallow poison or hug a dagger, my dear, to commit suicide. One can kill oneself and remain alive physically.'

Gallio rose, took her hand, and drew Cornelia to her feet. 'Dry your tears now, my love,' he said gently. 'When Marcellus comes, let him continue to be proud of you. There may be some trying days ahead for our son. Perhaps the memory of an intrepid mother will rearm him when he is low in spirit.'

'I shall try, Marcus.' Cornelia clung to him hungrily. It had been a long time since they had needed each other so urgently.

*   *   *   *   *   *

After Marcellus had spent a half-hour alone with his mother—an ordeal he had dreaded—his next engagement was with his sister. Their father had informed Lucia, and she had sent word by Tertia that she would be waiting for him in the pergola whenever it was convenient for him to come.

But first he must return to his rooms with the silk pillow his mother had insisted on giving him. It would be one more thing for Demetrius to add to their already cumbersome impedimenta, but it seemed heartless to refuse the present, particularly in view of the fine fortitude with which she had accepted their mutual misfortune. She had been tearful, but there had been no painful break-up of her emotional discipline.

Marcellus found the luggage packed and strapped for the journey, but Demetrius was nowhere to be found. Marcipor, who had appeared in the doorway to see if he might be of service, was questioned, and replied, with some reluctance and obvious perplexity, that he had seen Demetrius on his horse, galloping furiously down the driveway, fully an hour ago. Marcellus accepted this information without betraying his surprise. It was quite possible that the Greek had belatedly discovered the lack of some equipment necessary to their trip, and had set off for it without permission to do so. It was inconceivable that Demetrius would take advantage of this opportunity to make a dash for freedom. No, decided Marcellus, it wouldn't be that. But the incident needed explanation, for if Demetrius had gone for additional supplies he would not have strapped the luggage until his return.

Lucia was leaning against the balustrade, gazing toward the Tiber where little sails reflected final flashes of almost horizontal sunshine, and galleys moved so sluggishly they would have seemed not to be in motion at all but for the rhythmic dip of the long oars. One galley, a little larger than the others, was headed toward a wharf. Lucia shaded her eyes with her hands and was so intent upon the sinister black hulk that she did not hear Marcellus coming.

He joined her without words, and circled her girlish waist

tenderly. She slipped her arm about him, but did not turn her head. 'Might that be your galley?' she asked, pointing. 'It has three banks, I think, and a very high prow. Isn't that the kind that meets ships at Ostia?'

'That's the kind,' agreed Marcellus, pleased that the conversation promised to be dispassionate. 'Perhaps that is the boat.'

Lucia slowly turned about in his arms and affectionately patted his cheeks with her soft palms. She looked up, smiling resolutely, her lips quivering a little, but she was doing very well, her brother thought. He hoped his eyes were assuring her of his approval.

'I am so glad you are taking Demetrius,' she said, steadily. 'He wanted to go?'

'Yes,' replied Marcellus, adding after a pause, 'Yes, he really wanted to go.' They stood in silence for a little while, her fingers gently toying with the knotted silk cord at the throat of his tunic.

'All packed up?' Lucia was certainly doing a good job, they both felt. Her voice was well under control.

'Yes.' Marcellus nodded with a smile that meant everything was proceeding normally, just as if they were leaving on a hunting excursion. 'Yes, dear, all ready to go.' There was another longer interval of silence.

'Of course, you don't know—yet,' said Lucia, 'when you will be coming home.'

'No,' said Marcellus. After a momentary hesitation he added, 'Not yet.'

Suddenly Lucia uttered a long, agonized 'Oh!', wrapped her arms tightly around her brother's neck, buried her face against his breast, and shook with stifled sobs. Marcellus held her trembling body close.

'No, no,' he whispered. 'Let's see it through, precious child. It's not easy; but—well—we must behave like Romans, you know.'

Lucia stiffened, flung back her head, and faced him with streaming eyes aflame with anger.

'Like Romans!' she mocked. 'Behave like Romans! And what does a Roman ever get for being brave—and pretending it is fine—and noble —to give up everything—and make-believe it is glorious—glorious to suffer—and die—for Rome! For Rome! I hate Rome! Look what Rome has done for you—and all of us! Why can't we live in peace? The Roman Empire—Bah! What is the Roman Empire? A great swarm of slaves! I don't mean slaves like Tertia and Demetrius; I mean slaves like you and me—all our lives bowing and scraping and flattering ; our legions looting and murdering—and for what? To make Rome the capital of the world, they say! But why should the whole world be

ruled by a lunatic like old Tiberius and a drunken bully like Gaius? I
hate Rome! I hate it all!"

Marcellus made no effort to arrest the torrent, thinking it more
sensible to let his sister wear her passion out, and have done with it.
She hung limp in his arms now, her heart pounding hard.

'Feel better?' he asked, sympathetically. She slowly nodded against
his breast. Instinctively glancing about, Marcellus saw Demetrius
standing a few yards away with his face averted from them. 'I must
see what he wants,' he murmured, relaxing his embrace. Lucia slipped
from his arms and stared again at the river, unwilling to let the
imperturbable Greek see her so nearly overcome.

'The daughter of Legate Gallus is here, sir,' announced Demetrius.

'I can't see Diana now, Marcellus,' put in Lucia, thickly. 'I'll go
down through the gardens, and you talk to her.' She raised her voice
a little. 'Bring Diana to the pergola, Demetrius.' Without waiting for
her brother's approval, she walked rapidly toward the circular marble
stairway that led to the arbours and the pool. Assuming that his
master's silence confirmed the order, Demetrius was setting ff on his
errand. Marcellus recalled him with a quiet word and he ret. ᵈ his
steps.

'Do you suppose she knows?' asked Marcellus, frowning.

'Yes, sir.'

'What makes you think so?'

'The daughter of Legate Gallus appears to have been weeping, sir.'
Marcellus winced and shook his head.

'I hardly know what to say to her,' he confided, mostly to himself,
a dilemma that Demetrius made no attempt to solve. 'But,' Marcellus
sighed, 'I suppose I must see her.'

'Yes, sir,' said Demetrius, departing on his errand.

Turning toward the balustrade, Marcellus watched his siste s
dejected figure moving slowly through the arbours, and his heart ʸ as
suffused with pity. He had never seen Lucia so forlorn and und ʌe.
It was not surprising if she felt reluctant to meet Diana ir her
present state of collapse. Something told him that this impe ing
interview with Diana was likely to be difficult. He had not ofte ᵈeen
alone with her, even for a moment. This time they would not only be
alone, but in circumstances extremely trying. He was uncertain what
attitude he should take toward her.

She was coming now, out through the peristyle, walking with her
usual effortless grace, but lacking animation. It was unlike Demetrius
to send a guest to the pergola unattended, even though well aware
that Diana knew the way. Damn Demetrius!—he was behaving very

strangely this afternoon. Greeting Diana would be much more natural and unconstrained if he were present.

Marcellus sauntered along the pavement to meet her. It was true, as Lucia had said; Diana was growing up—and she was lovelier in this pensiveness than he had ever seen her. Perhaps the bad news had taken all the adolescent bounce out of her. But, whatever might account for it, Diana had magically matured. His heart speeded a little. The elder-brotherly smile with which he was preparing to welcome her seemed inappropriate if not insincere, and as Diana neared him, his eyes were no less sober than hers.

She gave him both hands, at his unspoken invitation, and looked up from under her long lashes, blinking back the tears and trying to smile. Marcellus had never faced her like this before, and the intimate contact stirred him. As he looked deeply into her dark eyes, it was almost as if he were discovering her; aware, for the first time, of her womanly contours, her finely sculptured brows, the firm but piquant chin, and the full lips—now parted with painful anxiety—disclosing even white teeth, grimly clenched.

'I am glad you came, Diana.' Marcellus had wanted this to sound fraternal, but it didn't. He was intending to add, 'Lucia will want to see you presently'—but he didn't; nor did he release her hands. It mystified him that she could stand still so long.

'Are you really going—to-night?' she asked, in a husky whisper.

Marcellus stared into her uplifted eyes, marvelling that the tempestuous, teasing, unpredictable Diana had suddenly become so winsome.

'How did you know?' he asked. 'Who could have told you so soon? I learned about it myself not more than three hours ago.'

'Does it matter—how I found out?' She hesitated, as if debating what next to say. 'I had to come, Marcellus,' she went on, bravely. 'I knew you would have no time—to come to me—and say good-bye.'

'It was very——' He stopped on the verge of 'kind,' which, he felt, would be too coolly casual, and saw Diana's eyes swimming with tears. 'It was very dear of you,' he said, tenderly. He clasped her hands more firmly and drew her closer. She responded, after a momentary reluctance.

'I wouldn't have done it, of course,' she said, rather breathlessly, 'if the time hadn't been so short. We're all going to miss you.' Then, a little unsteadily, she asked, 'Will I hear from you, Marcellus?' And when he did not immediately find words to express his happy surprise, she shook her head and murmured, 'I shouldn't have said that, I think. You will have more than enough to do. We can learn about each other through Lucia.'

'But I shall want to write to you, dear,' declared Marcellus, 'and you will write to me—often—I hope. Promise!'

Diana smiled mistily, and Marcellus watched her dimples deepen, and disappear. His heart skipped a beat when she whispered, 'You will write to me to-night? And send it back from Ostia—on the galley?'

'Yes, Diana!'

'Where is Lucia?' she asked, impetuously reclaiming her hands.

'Down in the arbours,' said Marcellus.

Before he realized her intention, Diana had run away. At the top of the stairs she paused to wave to him. He was on the point of calling to her to wait a moment, that he had something more to say; but the utter hopelessness of his predicament kept him silent. What more, he asked himself, did he want to say to Diana? What promise could he make to her, or exact of her? No; it was better to let this be their leave-taking. He waved her a kiss, and she vanished down the stairway. It was quite possible—quite probable, indeed—that he would never see Diana again.

Moodily, he started toward the house; then abruptly turned back to the pergola. The girls had met and were strolling, arm in arm, through the rose arbour. Perhaps he was having a final glimpse of his lovable young sister, too. There was no good reason why he should put Lucia to the additional pain of another farewell.

It surprised him to see Demetrius ascending the stairway. What errand could have taken him down to the gardens? wondered Marcellus. Perhaps he would explain without being questioned. His loyal Corinthian was not acting normally to-day. Presently he appeared at the top of the stairs and approached with the long, military stride that Marcellus had often found difficult to match when they were out on hunting trips. Demetrius seemed very well pleased about something; better than merely pleased. He was exultant! Marcellus had never seen such an expression on his slave's face.

'Shall I have the luggage taken down to the galley now, sir?' asked Demetrius, in a voice that betrayed recent excitement.

'Yes, if it is ready.' Marcellus was framing a question, but found it difficult, and decided not to pry. 'You may wait for me at the wharf,' he added.

'You will have had dinner, sir?'

Marcellus nodded; then suddenly changed his mind. He had taken leave of his family, one by one. They had all borne up magnificently. It was too much to ask of them—and him—that they should undergo a repetition of this distress in one another's presence.

'No,' he said, shortly. 'I shall have my dinner on the galley. You may arrange for it.'

'Yes, sir.' Demetrius's tone indicated that he quite approved of this decision.

Marcellus followed slowly toward the house. There were plenty of things he would have liked to do, if he had been given one more day. There was Tullus, for one. He must leave a note for Tullus.

* * * * * *

Upon meeting in the arbour, Lucia and Diana had both wept, wordlessly. Then they had talked in broken sentences about the possibilities of Marcellus's return, his sister fearing the worst, Diana wondering whether some pressure might be brought to bear on Gaius.

'You mean,' Lucia asked, 'that perhaps my father might——'

'No.' Diana shook her head decisively. 'Not your father. It would have to be done some other way.' Her eyes narrowed thoughtfully.

'Maybe your father could do something about it,' suggested Lucia.

'I don't know. Perhaps he might, if he were here. But his business in Marseilles may keep him stationed there until next winter.'

'You said good-bye to Marcellus?' asked Lucia, after they had walked on a little way in silence. She questioned Diana's eyes and smiled pensively as she watched the colour creeping up her cheeks. Diana nodded and pressed Lucia's arm affectionately, but made no other response.

'How did Demetrius get down here so fast?' she asked, impulsively. 'He came for me, you know, telling me Marcellus was leaving and wanted to see me. Just now I passed him. Don't tell me that slave was saying good-bye—like an equal?'

'It was rather strange,' admitted Lucia. 'Demetrius had never spoken to me in his life, except to acknowledge an order. I hardly knew what to make of it, Diana. He came out here, saluted with his usual formality, and delivered a little speech that sounded as if he had carefully rehearsed it. He said, "I am going away with the Tribune. I may never return. I wish to bid farewell to the sister of my master and thank her for being kind to her brother's slave. I shall remember her goodness." Then he took this ring out of his wallet——'

'Ring?' echoed Diana, incredulously. 'Keep still. Let me look at it,' she breathed. Lucia held up her hand, with fingers outspread, for a closer inspection in the waning light. 'Pretty, isn't it?' commented Diana. 'What is that device—a ship?'

'Demetrius said,' continued Lucia, ' "I should like to leave this with my master's sister. If I come back, she may return it to me. If I do not come back, it shall be hers. My father gave it to my mother. It is the only possession I was able to save.'"

'But—how queer!' murmured Diana. 'What did you say to him?'

'Well, what could I say?' Lucia's tone was self-defensive. 'After all, he is going away with my brother—at the risk of his own life. He's human, isn't he?'

'Yes, he's human,' agreed Diana, impatiently. 'Go on! What did you say?'

'I thanked him,' said Lucia, exasperatingly deliberate, 'and told him I thought it was wonderful of him—and I do think it was, Diana—to let me keep his precious ring; and—and—I said I hoped they would both come home safely—and I promised to take good care of his keepsake.'

'That was all right, I suppose,' nodded Diana, judicially. 'And—then what?' They had stopped on the tiled path, and Lucia seemed a little confused.

'Well,' she stammered, 'he was still standing there—and I gave him my hand.'

'You didn't!' exclaimed Diana. 'To a slave?'

'To shake, you know,' defended Lucia. 'Why shouldn' I ha been willing to shake hands with Demetrius? He's as clea as we re; certainly a lot cleaner than Bambo, who is always pawi me.'

'That's not the point, Lucia, whether Demetrius's h s are clean than Bambo's feet—and you know it. He is a slave, d we can't be too careful.' Diana's tone was distinctly stern, u il her curiosity overwhelmed her indignation. 'So—then,' she wen on, a little more gently, 'he shook hands with you.'

'No, it was ever so much worse than that.' Lucia grinned at the sight of Diana's shocked eyes. 'Demetrius took my hand, and put the ring on my finger—and then he kissed my hand—and—well, after all, Diana, he's going away with Marcellus —maybe to die for him! What should I have done? Slap him?'

Diana laid her hands on Lucia's shoulders and looked her squarely in the eyes.

'So then—after that—what happened?'

'Wasn't that enough?' parried Lucia, flinching a little from Diana's insistent search.

'Quite!' After a pause, she said, 'You're not expecting to wear that ring, are you, Lucia?'

'No. There's no reason why I should. It might get lost. And I don't want to hurt Tertia.'

'Is Tertia in love with Demetrius?'

'Mad about him! She has been crying her eyes out, this afternoon, the poor dear.'

'Does Demetrius know?'

'I don't see how he could help it.'

'And he doesn't care for her?'

'Not that way. I made him promise he would say good-bye to her.'

'Lucia, had it ever occurred to you that Demetrius has been secretly in love with you—maybe for a long time?'

'He has never given me any reason to think so,' replied Lucia, rather vaguely.

'Until to-day, you mean,' persisted Diana.

Lucia meditated an answer for a long moment.

'Diana,' she said, soberly, 'Demetrius is a slave. That is true. That is his misfortune. He was gently bred, in a home of refinement, and brought here in chains by ruffians who weren't fit to tie his sandals!' Her voice trembled with suppressed anger. 'Of course,' she went on, bitterly ironical, 'their being Romans made all the difference! So long as you're a Roman, you don't have to know anything—but pillage and bloodshed! Don't you realize, Diana, that everything in the Roman Empire to-day that any decent person would give a second thought was stolen from Greece? Tell me, how does it happen that we speak Greek, in preference to Latin? It's because the Greeks are leagues ahead of us, mentally. There's only one thing we do better: we're better butchers.'

Diana frowned darkly.

With her lips close to Lucia's ear, she said guardedly, 'You are a fool to say such things—even to me! It's too dangerous! Isn't your family in enough trouble? Do you want to see all of us banished—or in prison?'

* * * * * *

Marcellus stood alone at the rail of the afterdeck. He had not arrived at the wharf until a few minutes before the galley's departure; and, going up to the cramped and stuffy cabin to make sure his heavy luggage had been safely stowed, was hardly aware that they were out in the river until he came down and looked about. Already the long warehouse and the docks had retreated into the gloom, and the voices sounded far away.

High up on an exclusive residential hillside, two small points of light flickered. He identified them as the braziers at the eastern corners of the pergola. Perhaps his father was standing there at the balustrade.

Now they had passed the bend and the lights had disappeared. It was as if the first scroll of his life had now been written, read, and sealed.

The pink glow that was Rome had faded and the stars were brightening. Marcellus viewed them with a strange interest. They seemed like so many unresponsive spectators; not so dull-eyed and apathetic as the Sphinx, but calmly observant, winking occasionally to relieve the strain and clear their vision. He wondered whether they were ever moved to sympathy or admiration; or if they cared at all.

After a while he became conscious of the inexorable rasp of sixty oars methodically swinging with one obedience to the metallic blows of the boatswain's hammers as he measured their slavery on his huge anvil. . . . Click! Clack! Click! Clack!

Home—and Life—and Love made a final, urgent tug at his spirit. He wished he might have had an hour with Tullus, his closest friend. Tullus hadn't even heard what had happened to him. He wished he had gone back once more to see his mother. He wished he had kissed Diana. He wished he had not witnessed the devastating grief of his sister. . . . Click! Clack! Click! Clack!

He turned about and noticed Demetrius standing in the shadows near the ladder leading to the cabins. It was a comfort to feel the presence of his loyal slave. He decided to engage him in conversation; for the steady hammer-blows, down deep in the galley's hull, were beginning to pound hard in his temples. He beckoned. Demetrius approached and stood at attention. Marcellus made the impatient little gesture with both hands and a shake of the head which, by long custom, had come to mean, 'Be at ease! Be a friend!' Demetrius relaxed his stiff posture and drifted over to the rail beside Marcellus where he silently and without obvious curiosity waited his master's pleasure.

'Demetrius'—Marcellus swept the sky with an all-inclusive arm— 'do you ever believe in the gods?'

'If it is my master's wish, I do,' replied Demetrius, perfunctorily.

'No, no,' said Marcellus, testily, 'be honest. Never mind what I believe. Tell me what you think about the gods. Do you ever pray to them?'

'When I was a small boy, sir,' complied Demetrius, 'my mother taught us to invoke the gods. She was truly religious. There was a pretty statue of Priapus in our flower garden. I can still remember my mother kneeling there, on a fine spring day, with a little trowel in one hand and a basket of plants in the other. She believed that Priapus made things grow. . . . And my mother prayed to Athene every morning when my brothers and I followed the teacher into our school-room.' He was silent for a while; and then, prodded by an encouraging nod from Marcellus, he continued : 'My father offered libations to the

gods on their feast-days, but I think that was to please my mother.'
'This is most interesting—and touching, too,' observed Marcellus.
'But you haven't quite answered my question, Demetrius. Do you
believe in the gods—now?'
'No, sir.'
'Do you mean that you don't believe they render any service to men?
Or do you doubt that the gods exist at all?'
'I think it better for the mind, sir, to disbelieve in their existence.
The last time I prayed—it was on the day that our home was broken
up. As my father was led away in chains, I knelt by my mother and
we prayed to Zeus, the Father of gods and men, to protect his life.
But Zeus either did not hear us, or, hearing us, had no power to aid
us, or, having power to aid us, refused to do so. It is better, I think,
to believe that he did not hear us than to believe that he was unable
or unwilling to give aid. . . . That afternoon my mother went away—
upon her own invitation—because she could bear no more sorrow. . . .
I have not prayed to the gods since that day, sir. I have cursed and
reviled them, on occasion; but with very little hope that they might
resent my blasphemies. Cursing the gods is foolish and futile, I think.'
Marcellus chuckled grimly. This fine quality of contempt for the
gods surpassed any profanity he had ever heard. Demetrius had
spoken without heat. He had so little interest in the gods that he even
felt it was silly to curse them.
'You don't believe there is any sort of supernatural Intelligence in
charge of the universe?' queried Marcellus, gazing up into the sky.
'I have no clear thought about that, sir,' replied Demetrius, deliberately. 'It is difficult to account for the world without believing in a
Creator, but I do not want to think that the acts of men are inspired
by superhuman beings. It is better, I feel, to believe that men have
devised their brutish deeds without divine assistance.'
'I am inclined to agree with you, Demetrius. It would be a great
comfort, though, if (especially in an hour of bewilderment) one could
nourish a reasonable hope that a benevolent Power existed—somewhere
—and might be invoked.'
'Yes, sir,' conceded Demetrius, looking upward. 'The stars pursue
an orderly plan. I believe they are honest and sensible. I believe
in the Tiber, and in the mountains, and in the sheep and cattle and
horses. If there are gods in charge of them, such gods are honest and
sound of mind. But if there are gods on Mount Olympus, directing
human affairs, they are vicious and insane.' Apparently feeling
that he had been talking too much, Demetrius stiffened, drew himself
erect, and gave the usual evidences that he was preparing to get

back on his leash. But Marcellus wasn't quite ready to let him do so.

'Perhaps you think,' he persisted, 'that all humanity is crazy.'

'I do not know, sir,' replied Demetrius, very formally, pretending not to have observed his master's sardonic grin.

'Well,' hectored Marcellus, 'let's narrow it down to the Roman Empire. Do you think the Roman Empire is an insane thing?'

'Your slave, sir,' answered Demetrius, stiffly, 'believes whatever his master thinks about that.'

It was clear to Marcellus that the philosophical discussion was ended. By experience he had learned that once Demetrius resolved to crawl back into his slave status, no amount of coaxing would hale him forth. They both stood silently now, looking at the dark water swirling about the stern.

The Greek is right, thought Marcellus. That's what ails the Roman Empire, it is mad! That's what ails the whole world of men. *Mad!* If there is any Supreme Power in charge, He is *mad!* The stars are honest and sensible. But humanity is *insane!* . . . Click! Clack! Click! Clack!

Chapter III

AFTER the tipsy little ship had staggered down past the Lapari Islands in the foulest weather of the year, and had tacked gingerly through the perilous Strait of Messina, a smooth sea and a favourable breeze so eased Captain Manius's vigilance that he was available for a leisurely chat.

'Tell me something about Minoa,' urged Marcellus, after Manius had talked at considerable length about his many voyages: Ostia to Palermo and back, Ostia to Crete, to Alexandria, to Joppa.

Manius laughed, down deep in his whiskers.

'You'll find, sir, that there is no such place as Minoa.' And when Marcellus's stare invited an explanation, the swarthy navigator gave his passenger a lesson in history, some little of which he already knew.

Fifty years ago, the legions of Augustus had laid siege to the ancient city of Gaza, and had subdued it after a long and bitter campaign that had cost more than the conquest was worth.

'It would have been cheaper,' observed Manius, 'to have paid the high toll they demanded for travel on the salt trail.'

'But how about the Bedouins?' Marcellus wondered.

'Yes—and the Emperor could have bought off the Bedouins, too, for less than that war cost. We lost twenty-three thousand men, taking Gaza.'

Manius went on with the story. Old Augustus had been beside himself with rage over the stubborn resistance of the defence—composed of a conglomeration of Egyptians, Syrians, and Jews, none of whom were a bit squeamish at the sight of blood, who never took prisoners and were notoriously ingenious in the arts of torture. Their attitude, he felt, in wilfully defying the might of the Empire demanded that the old pest-hole Gaza should be cleaned up. Henceforth, declared Augustus, it was to be known as the Roman city of Minoa; and it was to be hoped that the inhabitants thereof, rejoicing in the benefits conferred upon them by a civilized state, would forget that there had ever been a municipality so dirty, unhealthy, quarrelsome, and altogether nasty as Gaza.

'But Gaza,' continued Manius, 'had been Gaza for seventeen centuries, and it would have taken more than an edict by Augustus to change its name.'

'Or its manners, either, I daresay,' commented Marcellus.

'Or its smell,' added Manius, dryly. 'You know, sir,' he went on, 'the crusty white shore of that old Dead Sea is like a salt lick beside a water-hole in the jungle where animals of all breeds and sizes gather and fight. This has been going on longer than any nation's history can remember. Occasionally some animal bigger than the others has appeared, driving all the rest of them away. Sometimes they have turned on the big fellow and chased him off, after which the little ones have gone to fighting again among themselves. Well—that's Gaza for you!'

'But the salt lick,' put in Marcellus, 'is not at Gaza, but at the Dead Sea.'

'Quite true,' agreed Manius, 'but you don't get to the Dead Sea for a lick at the salt unless Gaza lets you. For a long time the lion of Judah kept all the other animals away, after he had scared off the Philistine hyenas. Then the big elephant Egypt frightened away the lion. Then Alexander the tiger jumped on to the elephant. Always after a battle the little fellows would come sneaking back, and claw the hides off one another while the big ones were licking their wounds.'

'And what animal came after the tiger?' prodded Marcellus, though he knew the answer.

'The Roman eagle,' replied Manius. 'Flocks and swarms of Roman eagles, thinking to pick the bones; but there were plenty of survivors not ready to have their bones picked. That,' he interrupted himself to remark, 'was how we lost three-and-twenty thousand Romans—to get possession of the old salt lick.'

'That's how your master got into this predicament, Demetrius,' chuckled Marcellus ironically, 'by being bold.'

Apparently unwilling to discuss that unhappy circumstance, but wanting to support his end of the conversation, Demetrius said, 'Yes, sir,' so soberly that Marcellus laughed. Afterwards there was such a long hiatus that it was probable the Corinthian had dropped off to sleep, for the lazy roll of the little ship was an urgent sedative. Marcellus lay awake for an hour, consolidating the plan suggested by his shrewd and loyal Greek. Demetrius, he reflected, is right. If I am to command this fort at all, I must command it from the moment of my arrival. If they strike me down my exit will be at least honourable.

* * * * * *

It was well past mid-afternoon on the eighth day of March when Captain Manius manœuvred his unwieldly little tub through the busy roadstead of Gaza, and warped her flank against a vacant wharf. His duties at the moment were pressing, but he found time to say good-bye to the young Tribune with something of the sombre solicitude of the next of kin bidding farewell to the dying.

Demetrius had been among the early ones over the rail. After a while he returned with five husky Syrians, to whom he pointed out the burdens to be carried. There were no uniforms on the dirty wharf, but Marcellus was not disappointed. He had not expected to be met. The garrison had not been advised of his arrival. He would be obliged to appear at the fort unheralded.

Gaza was in no hurry, probably because of her great age and many infirmities. It was a full hour before enough pack asses were found to carry the baggage. Some more time was consumed in loading them. Another hour was spent moving at tortoise speed through the narrow, rough-cobbled, filthy streets, occasionally blocked by shrieking contestants for the right of way.

The Syrians had divined the Tribune's destination when they saw his uniform, and gave him a surly obedience. At length they were out on a busy, dusty highway, Marcellus heading the procession on a venerable, half-shed camel, led by the reeking Syrian with whom Demetrius—by pantomime—had haggled over the price of the expedition. This bargaining had amused Marcellus; for Demetrius, habitually quiet and reserved, had shouted and gesticulated with the best of them. Knowing nothing about the money of Gaza, or the rates for the service he sought, the Corinthian had fiercely objected to the Syrian's first three proposals, and had finally come to terms with savage mutters and scowls. It was difficult to recognize Demetrius in this new rôle.

Far ahead, viewed through the billowing clouds of yellow dust, appeared an immensely ugly twelve-acre square bounded by a high wall built of sun-baked brick, its corners dignified by tall towers. As they drew nearer, a limp Roman banner was identified, pendent from an oblique pole at the corner.

An indolent, untidy sentry detached himself from a villainous group of unkempt legionaries squatting on the ground, slouched to the big gate, and swung it open without challenging the party. Perhaps, thought Marcellus, the lazy lout had mistaken their little parade for a caravan that wanted to be convoyed. After they had filed through into the barren, sun-blistered courtyard, another sentry ambled down the steps of the praetorium and stood waiting until the Tribune's grunting camel had folded up her creaking joints. Demetrius, who had brought up the rear of the procession, dismounted from his donkey and marched forward to stand at his master's elbow. The sentry, whose curiosity had been stirred by the sight of the Tribune's insignia, saluted clumsily with a tarnished sword in a dirty hand.

'I am Tribune Marcellus Gallio!' The words were clipped and harsh. 'I am commissioned to take command of this fort. Conduct me to the officer in charge.'

'Centurion Paulus is not here, sir.'

'Where is he?'

'In the city, sir.'

'And when Centurion Paulus goes to the city, is there no one in command?'

'Centurion Sextus, sir; but he is resting, and has given orders not to be disturbed.'

Marcellus advanced a step and stared into the sulky eyes.

'I am not accustomed to waiting for men to finish their naps,' he growled. 'Obey me—instantly! And wash your dirty face before you let me see it again! What is this—a Roman fort, or a pigsty?'

Blinking a little, the sentry backed away for a few steps; and, turning, disappeared through the heavy doors. Marcellus strode heavily to and fro before the entrance, his impatience mounting. After wating for a few moments, he marched up the steps, closely followed by Demetrius, and stalked through the gloomy hall. Another sentry appeared.

'Conduct me to Centurion Sextus!' shouted Marcellus.

'By whose orders?' demanded the sentry, gruffly.

'By the orders of Tribune Marcellus Gallio, who has taken command of this fort. Lead on—and be quick about it!'

At that moment a near-by door opened and a burly, bearded figure emerged wearing an ill-conditioned uniform with a black eagle woven into the right sleeve of his red tunic. Marcellus brushed the sentry aside and confronted him.

'You are Centurion Sextus?' asked Marcellus; and when Sextus had nodded dully, he went on, ' I am ordered by Prince Gaius to command this fort. Have your men bring in my equipment.'

'Well—not so fast, not so fast,' drawled Sextus. 'Let's have a look at that commission.'

'Certainly.' Marcellus handed him the scroll; and Sextus, lazily unrolling it, held it close to his face in the waning light.

'I suggest, Centurion Sextus,' rasped Marcellus, 'that we repair to the Legate's quarters for this examination. In the country of which I am a citizen, there are certain courtesies——'.

Sextus grinned unpleasantly and shrugged.

'You're in Gaza now,' he remarked, half-contemptuously. 'In Gaza, you will find, we do things the easy way, and are more patient than our better-dressed equals in Rome. Incidentally,' added Sextus, dryly, as he led the way down the hall, 'I too am a Roman citizen.'

'How long has Centurion Paulus been in command here?' asked Marcellus, glancing about the large room into which Sextus had shown him.

'Since December. He took over temporarily, after the death of Legate Vitelius.'

'What did Vitelius die of?'

'I don't know, sir.'

'Not of wounds, then,' guessed Marcellus.

'No, sir. He had been ailing. It was a fever.'

'It's a wonder you're not all sick,' observed Marcellus, dusting his hands, distastefully. Turning to Demetrius he advised him to go out and stand guard over their equipment until it was called for.

Sextus mumbled some instructions to the sentry, who drifted away.

'I'll show you the quarters you may occupy until Commander Paulus returns,' he said, moving toward the door. Marcellus followed. The room into which he was shown contained a bunk, a table, and two chairs. Otherwise it was bare and grim as a prison cell. A door led into a smaller unfurnished cubicle.

'Order another bunk for this kennel,' growled Marcellus. 'My slave will sleep here.'

'Slaves do not sleep in the officers' row, sir,' replied Sextus, firmly.

'My slave does !'

'But it's against orders, sir!'

'There are no orders at this fort—but mine!' barked Marcellus.

Sextus nodded his head, and a knowing grin twisted his shaggy lips as he left the room.

*   *   *   *   *   *

It was a memorable evening at the fort. For years afterwards the story was retold until it had the flavour of a legend.

Marcellus, accompanied by his orderly, had entered the big mess-hall to find the junior officers seated. They did not rise, but there were no evidences of hostility in the inquisitive glances they turned in his direction as he made his way to the round table in the centre of the room. A superficial survey of the surrounding tables informed Marcellus that he was the youngest man present. Demetrius went directly to the kitchen to oversee his master's service.

After a while, Centurion Paulus arrived, followed by Sextus who had apparently waited to advise his chief of recent events. There was something of a stir when they came striding across the room to the centre table. Sextus mumbled an ungracious introduction. Marcellus rose and was ready to offer his hand, but Paulus did not see it; merely bowed, drew out his chair, and sat. He was not drunk, but it was evident that he had been drinking. His lean face, stubbly with a three-days' beard, was unhealthily ruddy; and his hands, when he began to gobble his food, were shaky. They were also dirty. And yet, in spite of his general appearance, Paulus bore marks of a discarded refinement. This man, thought Marcellus, may have been somebody, once upon a time.

'The new Legate, eh?' mumbled Paulus, with his mouth full. 'We have had no word of his appointment. However'—he waved a negligent hand, and helped himself to another large portion from the messy bowl of stewed meat—'we can go into that later; to-morrow, perhaps.' For some minutes he wolfed his rations, washing down the greasy meat with noisy gulps of a sharp native wine.

Having finished, Paulus folded his hairy arms on the table and stared insolently into the face of the young interloper. Marcellus met his cloudy eyes steadily. Each knew that the other was taking his measure, not only as to height and weight—in which dimensions they were approximately matched, with Paulus a few pounds heavier, perhaps, and a few years older—but, more particularly, appraising each other's timbre and temper. Paulus grimaced unpleasantly.

'Important name—Gallio,' he remarked, with mock deference. 'Any relation to the rich Senator?'

'My father,' replied Marcellus, coolly.

'Oh-oh!' chuckled Paulus. 'Then you must be one of these club-house swiftly, with as much audacity as if he had earned this more stable footing, and endeavoured to force Marcellus into further retreat. But on that spot the battle was permanently settled. Paulus tried everything he could recall, dodging, crouching, feinting—and all the time growing more and more fatigued. Now his guard was becoming sluggish and increasingly vulnerable. Twice, the spectators noted, it would have been simple enough for the Tribune to have ended the affair.

And now, with a deft manœuvre, Marcellus brought the engagement to a dramatic close. Studying his opportunity, he thrust the tip of his broadsword into the hilt-housing of Paulus's wearied weapon, and tore it out of his hand. It fell with a clatter to the stone floor. Then there was a moment of absolute silence. Paulus stood waiting. His posture did him credit, all thought; for, though his face showed the shock of this stunning surprise, it was not the face of a coward. Paulus was decisively defeated, but he had better stuff in him than any of them had supposed.

Marcellus stooped and picked up the fallen broadsword by its tip, drew back his arm with the slow precision of a careful aim, and sent it swiftly, turning end over end through the mess-hall, to the massive wooden door, where it drove its weight deep into the timber with a resounding thud. Nobody broke the stillness that followed. Marcellus then reversed his own sword in his hand, again took a deliberate aim, and sent the heavy weapon hurtling through the air towards the same target. It thudded deep into the door close beside the sword of Paulus.

The two men faced each other silently. Then Marcellus spoke; firmly but not arrogantly.

'Centurion Paulus,' he said, 'you will now apologize for conduct unbecoming an officer.'

Paulus shifted his weight and drew a long breath; half-turned to face the tightening ring of spectators; then straightened defiantly, folded his arms, and sneered.

Marcellus deliberately drew his dagger from his belt, and stepped forward. Paulus did not move.

'You had better defend yourself, Centurion,' warned Marcellus. 'You have a dagger, have you not? I advise you to draw it!' He advanced another step. 'Because—if you do not obey my order—I intend to kill you!'

It was not easy for Paulus, but he managed to do it adequately. Demetrius remarked afterwards that it was plain to be seen that Centurion Paulus was not an accomplished orator, which Marcellus thought was a very droll comment.

After Paulus had stammered through his glum impromptu speech,

Marcellus responded, 'Your apology is accepted, Centurion. Now perhaps there is something else that you might think it timely to say to your fellow officers. I have not yet been officially presented to them. As the retiring Commander, it is, I feel, your right to extend this courtesy.'

Paulus fully found his voice this time, and his announcement was made in a firm tone.

'I am introducing Tribune Marcellus Gallio, the Legate of this legion, and Commander of this fort.'

There was a concerted clatter of swords drawn in salute—all but the sword of paunchy old Sextus, who pretended to be adjusting his harness.

'Centurion Sextus!' called Marcellus, sharply. 'Bring me my sword!'

All eyes watched Sextus plod awkwardly over to the big door and tug the sword out of the thick planking.

'Bring the sword of Centurion Paulus, also!' commanded Marcellus.

Sextus worked the second broadsword out of the timber, and came with heavy feet and a dogged air. Marcellus took the heavy weapons, handed Paulus his, and waited to receive Sextus's salute. The hint was taken without further delay. Paulus also saluted before sheathing his sword.

'We will now finish our dinner,' said Marcellus, coolly. 'You will restore the tables to their places. Breakfast will be served to the staff to-morrow morning at five. All officers will be smooth-shaven. There will be an inspection on the parade-ground at six, conducted by Lieutenant-Commander Paulus. That will do.'

Paulus had asked, respectfully enough, to be excused as they returned to their table, and Marcellus had given him permission to go. Sextus was trailing along after him, without asking leave; and upon being sharply asked if he had not forgotten something, mumbled that he had finished his dinner.

'Then you will have time,' said Marcellus, 'to clear the Commander's quarters, so that I may occupy those rooms to-night.'

Sextus acknowledged the order and tramped heavily to the door. Appetites were not keen, but the staff made a show of finishing dinner. Marcellus lingered at his table. At length, when he rose, they all stood in their places. He bowed and left the room, followed by Demetrius. As they passed the open door of the Commander's rooms, on their way to the quarters which had been assigned them earlier, it was observed that a dozen slaves were busily engaged in making the place ready for occupation.

After a few minutes, the men came and transferred their various gear to the Commander's quarters. When they were alone, Marcellus sat down behind the big desk. Demetrius stood at attention before him.

'Well, Demetrius?' Marcellus raised his brows inquiringly. 'What is on your mind?'

Demetrius brought the shaft of his spear to his forehead in salute. 'I wish to say, sir, that I am much honoured to be the slave of the Commander of Minoa.'

'Thanks, Demetrius,' smiled Marcellus, wearily. 'We will have to wait—and see—who commands Minoa. This is a tough undertaking. The preliminary skirmish was satisfactory, but—making peace is always more difficult than making war.'

For the next few days the nerves of the legion were tense. The new Legate had demonstrated his determination to be in full authority, but it was by no means clear whether that authority would be maintained on any other terms than a relentless coercion.

Paulus had suffered a severe loss of prestige, but his influence was still to be reckoned with. He was obeying orders respectfully, but with such grim taciturnity that no one was able to guess what was going on in his mind. Whether he was not yet fully convalescent from the wounds dealt to his pride, or was sullenly deliberating some overt act of revenge, remained to be seen. Marcellus had formed no clear opinion about this. Demetrius planted his bunk directly inside the door, every night, and slept with his dagger in his hand.

After a week, the tension began to relax a little as the garrison became accustomed to the new discipline. Marcellus issued crisp orders and insisted upon absolute obedience; not the sluggish compliance that had been good enough for Gaza, but a prompt and vigorous response that marched with clipped steps and made no tarrying to ask foolish questions or offer lame excuses.

It had seemed wise to the new Commander to let his more personal relations with the staff develop naturally without too much cultivation. He showed no favouritism, preserved his official dignity, and in his dealings with his fellow officers wasted no words. He was just, considerate, and approachable, but very firm. Presently the whole organization was feeling the effect of the tighter regulations, but without apparent resentment. The men marched with a fresh vigour and seemed to take pride in keeping their equipment in order. The appearance and morale of the officers had vastly improved.

Every morning, Paulus, now second in command, came to the office of Marcellus for instructions. Not a word had passed between them relative to their dramatic introduction. Their conversations were conducted with icy formality and the stiffest kind of official courtesy.

Paulus, faultlessly dressed, would appear at the door and ask to see the Commander. The sentry would convey the request. The Commander would instruct the sentry to admit the Centurion. Paulus would enter and stand straight as an arrow before the official desk. Salutes would be exchanged.

'It is necessary to replace six camels, sir.'

'Why?' Marcellus would snap.

'One is lame. Two are sick. Three are too old for service.'

'Replace them!'

'Yes, sir.'

The Paulus would salute and stalk out. Sometimes Marcellus wondered whether this frosty relationship was to continue for ever. He hoped not. He was feeling lonely in the remote altitude to which he had climbed in order to maintain discipline. Paulus was, he felt, an excellent fellow; embittered by this exile, and morally disintegrated by the boredom and futility of his desert life. Marcellus had resolved that if Paulus showed the slightest inclination to be friendly, he would meet the overture halfway; but not a step farther. Nor would he take the initiative.

As for Sextus, Marcellus had very little direct contact with him, for Sextus received his orders through Paulus. The big, gruff fellow had been punctilious in his obedience, but very glum. At the mess-table he had nothing to say; ate his rations with a scowl, and asked to be excused.

One evening, after ten days had passed, Marcellus noticed that Sextus's chair was vacant.

'Where is he?' demanded the Commander, nodding toward the unoccupied place.

'Broke his leg, sir,' answered Paulus.

'When?'

'This afternoon, sir.'

'How?'

'Stockade gate fell on him, sir.'

Marcellus immediately rose and left the table. After a moment, Paulus followed and overtook him on the way to Sextus's quarters. They fell into step, and marched side by side with long strides.

'Bad break?'

'Clean break. Upper leg. Not much mangled.'

Sextus was stretched out on his back, beads of sweat on his forehead. He glanced up and made an awkward gesture of greeting.

'Much pain?' inquired Marcellus.

'No, sir.' Sextus gritted his teeth.

'Gallant liar!' snapped Marcellus. 'Typical Roman lie! You wouldn't admit you were in pain if you'd been chopped to mincemeat! That bunk is bad; sags like a hammock. We will find a better one. Have you had your dinner?'

Sextus shook his head; said he didn't want anything to eat.

'Well—we'll see about that!' said Marcellus, gruffly.

By inspection hour next morning, the story had spread through the acres of brown tents that the new Commander—who had had them all on the jump and had strutted about through the camp with long legs and a dark frown—had gone to the kitchen of the officers' mess and had concocted a nourishing broth for old Sextus; had moved him to airier quarters; had supervised the making of a special bed for him.

That day Marcellus became the Commander of the fort at Minoa. That night Demetrius did not take his dagger to bed with him; he didn't even bother to lock the door.

*   *   *   *   *   *

The next morning, Paulus pushed the sentry aside at the Commander's quarters and entered without more ceremony than a casual salute. Marcellus pointed to a vacant chair and Paulus accepted it.

'Hot day, Centurion Paulus,' remarked Marcellus.

'Gaza does not believe in pleasant weather, sir. The climate suits the temper of the people. It's either hot or cold.' Paulus tipped back his chair and thrust his thumbs under his belt. 'The Jews have an important festival, sir. They observe it for a week when the moon is full in the month they call Nisan. Perhaps you know about it.'

'No, never heard of it,' admitted Marcellus. 'Is it any of our business?'

'It's their annual Passover Week,' explained Paulus, 'celebrating their flight from Egypt.'

'What have they been doing down in Egypt?' asked Marcellus indifferently.

'Nothing—lately,' grinned Paulus. 'This happened fifteen centuries ago.'

'Oh—that! Do they still remember?'

'The Jews never forget anything, sir. Every year at this season, all the Jews who can possibly get there go to Jerusalem to "eat the Passover," as their saying is; but most of them are quite as much interested in family reunions, games, sports, auctions, and all manner of shows. Caravans of merchandise come from afar to market their wares. Thousands crowd the city and camp in the surrounding hills. It is a lively spectacle, sir.'

'You have been there, it seems.'

'On each of the eleven years since I was sent to this fort, sir,' nodded Paulus. 'The Procurator in Jerusalem—I think you know that his office outranks all of the other Palestinian establishments—expects detachments from the forts at Capernaum, Cæsarea, Joppa, and Minoa to come and help keep order.'

'An unruly crowd, then?' surmised Marcellus.

'Not very, sir. But always, when so many Jews assemble, there is the usual talk of revolution. They wail sad chants and prattle about their lost heritage. So far as I know, this unrest has never amounted to anything more alarming than a few street brawls. But the Procurator thinks it is a good thing, on these occasions, to have a conspicuous display of Roman uniforms—and a bit of drill-work in the vicinity of the Temple.' Paulus chuckled, reminiscently.

'Do we get a formal notice?'

'No, sir. The Procurator does not trouble himself to send a courier. He takes it for granted that a detachment from Minoa will attend.'

'Very well, Paulus. How many men do we send, and when do they go?'

'A company, sir; a full hundred. It is a three-day journey. We should start the day after to-morrow.'

'You may arrange for it then, Paulus. Would you like to command the detachment, or have you had enough of it!'

'Enough of it! By no means, sir! This expedition is the only bright event of the year! And if I may venture to suggest, Tribune, you yourself might find this a most refreshing diversion.'

'On your recommendation, I shall go. What is the nature of the equipment?'

'It is not very burdensome, sir. Because it is a gala occasion, we carry our best uniforms. You will be proud of your command, I think; for it is a reward of merit here to be chosen for this duty, and the men are diligent in polishing their weapons. Otherwise we pack nothing but provisions for tenting and meals on the way. We are housed in commodious barracks in Jerusalem, and the food is of an uncommonly fine quality, furnished by certain rich men of the city.'

'What?' Marcellus screwed up his face in surprise. 'Do they not resent Roman rule in Jerusalem?'

Paulus laughed ironically.

'It is the common people who feel the weight of the Roman yoke, sir. As for the rich, many of whom collect the tribute for Tiberius— and keep a quarter of it for themselves—they are quite content. Oh, publicly, of course, the nabobs have to make a show of lamenting the loss of their kingdom; but these fat old merchants and money-lenders would be quite upset if a real revolution got started. You will find that the city fathers and the Procurator are thick as thieves, though they pretend to be at odds.'

'But this is amazing, Paulus! I had always supposed that the Jews were passionately patriotic, and uncompromising in their bitter hatred of the Empire.'

'That is quite true, sir, of the common people. Very zealous, indeed! They keep hoping for their old independence. Doubtless you have heard of their ancient myth about a Messiah.'

'No. What's a Messiah?'

'The Messiah is their deliverer, sir. According to their prophets, he will appear, one day, and organize the people to achieve their freedom.'

'I never heard of it,' admitted Marcellus, indifferently. 'But small wonder. I haven't had much interest in religious superstitions.'

'Nor I!' protested Paulus. 'But one hears a good deal about this Messiah business during Passover Week.' He laughed at the recollection. 'Why, sir, you should see them! Sleek, paunchy old fellows, swathed from their whiskers to their sandals in voluminous black robes, stalking through the streets, with their heads thrown back and their eyes closed, beating their breasts and bleating about their lost kingdom and bellowing for their Messiah! Pouf! They don't want any other kingdom than the one that stuffs their wallets and their bellies. They don't want a Messiah—and if they thought there was the slightest likelihood of a revolution against Roman domination they would be the first to stamp it out.'

'They must be a precious lot of hypocrites!' growled Marcellus.

'Yes, sir,' agreed Paulus, 'but they set a fine table!'

For a little while, the Tribune sat silently shaking his head in glum disgust.

'I know the world is full of rascality, Paulus, but this beats anything I ever heard of!'

'It is rather sickening, sir,' conceded Paulus. 'The sight that always makes me want to slip a knife under one of those pious arms, upraised in prayer, is the long procession of the poor and sick and blind and crippled trailing along after one of these villainous old frauds, under the impression that their holy cause is in good hands.' He interrupted himself to lean over the arm of his chair for a better view of the doorway, and caught sight of Demetrius standing in the hall within sound of their voices. Marcellus's eyes followed.

'My Greek slave keeps his own counsel, Centurion,' he said, in a confidential tone. 'You need not fear that he will betray any private conversation.'

'What I was going to say, sir,' continued Paulus, lowering his voice, 'this political situation in Jerusalem, revolting as it sounds, is not unusual.' He leaned halfway across the desk, and went on in a guarded whisper, 'Commander, that's what holds the Empire together! If it were not for the rich men in all our subjugated provinces—men whose avarice is greater than their local patriotism—the Roman Empire would collapse!'

'Steady, Paulus!' warned Marcellus. 'That's a dangerous theory to expound! You might get into trouble—saying such things.'

Paulus stiffened with sudden wrath.

'Trouble!' he snarled, bitterly. 'I did get into trouble, sir, that way! I was fool enough to be honest in the presence of Germanicus! That,' he added, only half audibly, 'was how I—a Legate—earned my passage to Minoa to become a Centurion! But, by the gods, what I said was true! The Roman Empire was consolidated, and is now supported, by the treachery of rich provincials, willing to betray their own people! This strategy is not original with us, of course! Rome learned the trick from Alexander. He learned it from the Persians, who had learned it in Egypt. Buy up the big men of a little country and—pouf!—you can have the rest of them for nothing!' Paulus's face was flushed with anger, and after his seditious speech he sat with clenched hands, flexing the muscles of his jaw. Then he faced Marcellus squarely, and muttered, 'Valour of Rome! Bah! I spit on the valour of Rome! Valour of treachery! Valour of gold! Valour of hurling the poor at one another on the battlefield, while the big ones are off in a corner selling them out! The great and proud Roman Empire!' Paulus brought his fist down with a bang on the desk. 'I spit on the Roman Empire!'

'You are very indiscreet, Paulus,' said Marcellus, seriously. 'For remarks of that sort, you could have your pelt pulled off. I hope you do not often let yourself go like that.'

Paulus rose and hitched up his broad belt.

'I had no fear of speaking my mind to you, sir,' he said.

'Why are you so sure that I wouldn't give you away?' asked Marcellus.

'Because,' replied Paulus, confidently, 'you believe in real valour—the kind that demands courage!'

Marcellus answered with an appreciative smile.

'It is a wonder, Paulus,' he said, thoughtfully, 'that the ordinary rank and file do not take things into their own hands.'

'Pouf! What can they do?' scoffed Paulus, with a shrug. 'They're nothing but sheep, with no shepherd! Take these Jews, for example: now and then, some fiery fellow goes howling mad over the raw injustice, and gets up on a cart, and lets out a few shrieks—but they dispose of him in a hurry!'

'Who shuts him up? The rich men?'

'Well, not directly. It is we who are always called in to do the dirty work. It's obvious that Rome can't permit such uprisings, but it is the rich and greedy provincials who nip revolutions in the bud.'

'Damned scoundrels!' exclaimed Marcellus.

'Yes, sir,' assented Paulus, his gusty storm having blown out, 'but you will find that these damned scoundrels in Jerusalem know good wine when they see it, and aren't mean about sharing it with the Roman legions. That,' he added, with cool mockery, 'is to encourage us to be on the look-out for any foolhardy patriot who squeaks about the lost kingdom!'

Chapter IV

THE first day's journey, from Gaza to Ascalon, was intolerably tedious, for the deep-rutted highway was crowded with creeping caravans and filthy with dust.

'It will be better to-morrow,' promised Melas, amused by the grotesque appearance of Demetrius who had rewound his turban about his face until only his eyes were visible.

'Let us hope so!' grumbled the Corinthian, tugging at the lead-donkey that was setting off toward a clump of thistles. 'But how will it be better? These snails are all crawling to Jerusalem, are they not?'

'Yes, but we leave the highway at Ascalon,' explained Melas, 'and take a shorter road through the hills. The caravans do not travel it. They're afraid of the Bedouins.'

'And we aren't?'

'We're too many for them. They wouldn't risk it.'

Centurion Paulus's stocky, bow-legged, red-headed Thracian was enjoying himself. Not often was Melas in a position to inform his betters; and, observing that the status of Demetrius was enviable compared to his own, it had made him quite expansive to be on such friendly terms with the new Legate's well-spoken slave.

'It isn't the camels that stir up the dust,' advised Melas, out of his long experience. 'Your camel lifts his big padded paws and lays them down on top of the soft dirt. It's the asses that drag their feet. But I hate camels!'

'I am not very well acquainted with camels,' admitted Demetrius, willing to show some interest in his education.

'Nobody is,' declared Melas. 'You can live with a camel for years, and treat him as your brother, but you can never trust him. See that?' He tapped a badly disfigured nose. 'I got that up in Gaul, a dozen years ago. The fleas and flies were driving my master's old Menepthah crazy. I spent the better part of two days rubbing olive oil into his mangy hide. And he stood like a rock, and purred like a cat; because he liked it. When I was tired out, he turned around and kicked me in the face.'

Demetrius laughed, as was expected, and inquired what sort of revenge Melas had considered appropriate, a query that delighted him, for there was more of the story.

'I was so blind mad,' continued Melas, 'that I did the same thing to him—only Menepthah saw it coming and grabbed my foot. Ever have a camel bite you? Now, an ass,' he expounded, 'or a dog, will snap and nip and nibble at you; but if he is going to bite, he tells you. Your camel never lets you into the secret. When he bites, nobody knows what is in his mind—but himself. I was laid up for two weeks, the time Menepthah bit my foot. I don't like camels,' he added, reasonably enough, his new friend thought.

'They can't be blamed much for wanting to get even,' observed Demetrius. 'It's a pretty rough life, I suppose.'

Melas seemed to be weighing this bland comment on his not very sensitive scales as they trudged along, and presently gave Demetrius a long, appraising look out of the tail of his eye. His lip curled in a sour grin. At length he ventured to give his thoughts an airing; having a care, however, to keep them on a leash.

'It doesn't do much good—trying to get even. Take your slave now; he can't get anywhere that way. Camels and asses and slaves are better off minding their masters.' And when Demetrius did not comment, Melas added, encouragingly, 'Or—don't you think so?'

Demetrius nodded, without interest. He had no desire to discuss this matter.

'If you're going to serve another man, at all,' he remarked casually, 'it's only good sense to serve him well.'

'That's what I always say,' approved Melas, with such exaggerated innocence that Demetrius wondered whether the fellow was making a smug pretence of lily-white loyalty—or recklessly toying with a piece of crude irony. He thought it might be interesting to find out.

'Of course, slavery is a bit different from the employment of freedmen,' experimented Demetrius. 'If a freedman finds his work distasteful he can leave it, which is ever so much better than keeping on at it, and shirking it. The slave does not have this choice.'

Melas chuckled a little.

'Some slaves,' he remarked, 'are like asses. They snap at their masters, and get slapped for it. They sit down and balk, and get themselves whipped and kicked. There's no sense in that. And then there are some slaves that behave like camels; just keep going on, and taking it, no matter how they're used '—Melas's tone was getting noticeably metallic, to match his heavy scowl—'and one day—when the master is drunk, maybe—the poor beast pays him out.'

'And then what?' demanded Demetrius.

Melas shrugged, sullenly.

'Then he'd better run away,' he concluded. Presently he muttered an afterthought. ' Not much chance for a camel. Once in a while a slave gets away. Three years ago——' Melas lowered his voice, though there was no need of this precaution as they were far at the rear of the procession, and the furtive quality of the Thracian's tone hinted at a conspiratorial confidence. 'It was on this same trip—three years ago. Commander Vitelius's slave, as cheerful and obedient as anybody you ever met—Sevenus, by name—managed to lose himself the next to the last day in Jerusalem. Nobody knows what became of him.' Melas stepped nearer and muttered out of the corner of his mouth. 'No, y ut me. Sevenus left for Damascus. Wanted me to go with him. Sometimes I've wished I had taken the chance. It's easy enough. W e more or less on our own in Jerusalem. The officers give themselves good time. Don't want the slaves hanging about. Bad for discip ne Melas winked significantly. 'The Centurions like to play a little.'

Demetrius listened without comment to this lengthy speech and Melas, a bit anxious, searched his eyes for advice as to the sa y of occeding farther.

'Of course, it's no secret,' he proclaimed, doffing his air of mystery. verybody at Minoa knows about it—all but what I just to you.'

Demetrius knew he was making a mistake when he asked the uestion hat implied a personal interest in this matter, but the story h stirred his curiosity.

'What made this fellow Sevenus think he had a chance of freedom in Damascus?'

Melas's eyes relighted.

'Why, Damascus is Syrian. Those people up there hate Rome like poison! The old city's full of Roman slaves, they say; living right out in the open, too; making no attempt to hide. Once you get there, you're safe as a bug in a donkey's ear.'

* * * * * *

Early next morning, their caravan broke camp and moved off through the bare hills over a winding road which narrowed frequently, in long ravines and deep waddies, to a mere bridle-path that ravelled out yesterday's compact pilgrimage into a single thread.

It was a desolate country, practically uninhabited. Small herds of wild goats, almost indistinguishable from the jagged brown rocks on the treeless hillsides, grouped to stare an absurd defiance of any attempted trespass upon their domain. In the valleys, the spring rains had fraudulently invited an occasional tuft of vegetation to believe it had a chance of survival. Beside a blistered water-hole a brave little clump of violets drooped with thirst.

Demetrius was finding pleasure in this stage of the journey. The landscape was uninspiring, but it refreshed his spirit to be out in the open and at a comfortable distance from the uncouth Melas, whose favourite topic had become disquieting. There was little doubt but the Thracian was building up toward a proposal of escape; either that, or was harbouring an even more sinister design to engage him in a conspiracy and then expose him. Of course, this suspicion might be quite unfair to the fellow; but it would be dangerous to take any risks. No matter what he himself might say to Melas, on this touchy matter, i could easily become a weapon in the garrulous Thracian's hand, if he happened to be upset about something or made envious of the unusual privileges accorded to the Commander's more fortunate slave. Deme trius had resolved to be painstakingly prudent in any conversation with Melas, and as much as possible avoid being alone with him. Beside there was much to think about, left over from a discussion betwe Marcellus and Paulus, last night; a most provocative—and high amusing—survey of the gods, conducted by two men who had no pi at all. A good deal of it had been shockingly irreverent, but undenia entertaining.

Late yesterday afternoon, when the company had halted near spring (on city property, a mile north-east of Ascalon) Demetrius ha been happy to receive a summons to attend his master, for he had begun to feel lonely and degraded. He was amazed at the smart appearance of the camp. Almost by magic the brown tents had risen in four precise rows, the commissary had unpacked and set up its field equipment, chairs and tables and bunks had been unfolded and put in order. Banners were flying. Sentries were posted. The local Roman representative—a seedy, unprepossessing old fellow, with the bright pink nose of a seasoned winebibber—accompanied by three obsequious Jewish merchants, came out to read and present an illuminated scroll which eloquently (and untruthfully) certified to Ascalon's delight that the famed Legion of Minoa had deigned to accept the city's poor but cheerful hospitality. They had brought with them four huge wineskins bulging with the best of the native product, and were invited to remain for supper, after the Commander had formally replied (with his staff ranged stiffly to the rear of him) that Minoa was fully as glad to be in Ascalon as Ascalon was to entertain Minoa, which his slave considered deliciously droll.

After the evening meal had been disposed of, and his immediate duties performed, Demetrius had stretched out on the ground in the shadow of the Commander's tent—a quite imposing tent, larger than the others, trimmed with red flouncing, red silk curtains at the entrance and a canopy over the doorway supported by slanting spear-shafts. With his fingers interlaced behind his head, Demetrius lay gazing up at the stars, marvelling at their uncommon brightness, and effortlessly listening to the subdued voices of his master and Paulus, lounging in camp-chairs under the gaudy canopy. Apparently the visitation of the local dignitaries, who had now left for home, accounted for the conversation. Paulus was holding forth with the leisurely drawl of an amateur philosopher—benign, tolerant, and a little bit tight. Demetrius cocked an ear. Occasionally, in such circumstances, a man imprudently spoke his honest convictions about something; and, if Paulus had any convictions, it might be interesting to learn what they were.

'The Jews,' Paulus was saying, 'are a queer people. They admit it themselves; brag about it, in fact; there are no other people like them in the world. For one thing, they're under a special divine protection. Their god, Jehovah—they have only one, you know—isn't interested in anybody else but the Jews. Of course, there would be nothing positively immoral about that belief, if it weren't for the fact that their Jehovah created the world and all its inhabitants, but has no use for any of the other people; says the Jews are his children. Presumably the rest of the world can look out for itself. If they'd just admit that Jehovah was a sort of local deity——'

'Oh, but we do the same thing, Paulus, don't we?' rejoined Marcellus. 'Isn't Jupiter a sort of general superintendent of the universe, with unlimited jurisdiction?'

'Not at all; not at all, sir,' protested Paulus, lazily. 'Jupiter hasn't any interest in the Egyptians, but he doesn't claim he made them what they are, and then despise them for being no better. And he never said that the Syrians are a lousy lot, for not lighting bonfires on his feast-day. And Jupiter never said he was going to see that the Romans had the best of it—all the time.'

'Did Jehovah say that to the Jews?'

Demetrius laughed silently. He had suspected that Marcellus wasn't very well informed about the various religions, but his master's almost complete ignorance on the subject was ludicrous.

'Why, certainly!' Paulus was orating. 'Started them off in a garden where he had grown a fruit they were forbidden to eat. Of course they ate it, not to satisfy their hunger but their curiosity.'

'One would think Jehovah might have been delighted over their curiosity,' put in Marcellus, 'seeing that every good thing we have was discovered through someone's inquisitiveness.'

'Yes, but this made Jehovah angry,' explained Paulus, 'so he pitched them out into the desert, and let them get tricked into slavery. Then he told them how to escape, and turned them loose in a wilderness. Then he promised them a land of their own——'

'And this is it!' laughed Marcellus. 'What a promised land!'

'There isn't a more worthless strip of country in the world!' declared Paulus. 'And now the Jews have lost control of it. You'd think that after about fifteen hundred years of hard knocks, poverty, and slavery, these specially favoured children of Jehovah would begin to wonder whether they might not be better off without so much divine attention.'

'Perhaps that accounts for this Messiah business that you spoke about the other day. Maybe they've given up hope that Jehovah will take care of them, and think the Messiah might improve their fortunes when he comes. Do you suppose that's what they have in mind? It's not unreasonable. I daresay that's the way we and the Greeks accumulated so many gods, Paulus. When one god gets weary and impotent, another fresher god takes over. Didn't old Zeus retire once in favour of his son Apollo?'

'Not for long,' remembered Paulus. 'Apparently the weather hadn't been very good, so young Apollo decided he would manage the sun; and ran amuck with it. Old Zeus had to straighten out the tangle for the boy. Now, there's sense in a religion like that, Tribune. Our gods behave the way we do, naturally, because we made them the way we are. Everybody gets tired of the dictatorial old man, and eventually he gets tired too; decides to let his son run the business—whether it's growing gourds or managing the planets; but he never thinks the young fellow is competent, so he keeps on interfering until presently there is a row. That's why our religion is such a comfort to us,' Paulus continued, elaborately ironical.

'I'm afraid you're not very pious,' commented Marcellus. 'If the gods hear what you are saying, they may not like it. They might think you doubted their reality.'

'Not at all, sir! It's men like me who really believe in their reality.

They're authentic—the gods! Some of them want war, some want peace, some of them don't know what they want—except an annual feast-day and a big parade. Some give you rest and sleep, some drive you insane. Some you are expected to admire, and some you are expected to hate, and all of them are never quite happy unless they are frightening you and assured that you are afraid. This is sensible. This is the way life is! . . . But these Jews! There they are, with only one god; and he is perpetually right, perpetually good, wise, loving. Of course he is stubborn, because they are stubborn; doesn't approve of pleasure, because they never learned how to play; never makes any mistakes, because the Jew never makes any mistakes. Tribune, Jehovah can't help being a pessimist. The Jews are a pessimistic people.'

'Maybe Jehovah thinks it is a good thing for his children to endure hardship,' speculated Marcellus; 'toughens their fibre, knocks off their surplus fat, keeps them in fighting trim. I believe he has a good idea there, Paulus. Sometimes I've thought that Rome would be better off if we patricians had to scratch for a living, and stole less from the neighbours.'

There was a considerable pause at this point in the sacrilegious discussion and Demetrius had wondered whether they hadn't about exhausted themselves and their subject. But not quite.

'Rome will have that problem solved for her, one of these days,' Paulus was muttering, ominously. 'The sceptre is passed around, Commander. Egypt has her day in the sunshine. Darius tramps about, scaring everybody for an hour or two. Alexander sobs because there's no one left to be subdued. The Cæsars drive their chariots over Alexander's world; so drunk with power that they can't even bear to let these poor Hebrews own a few acres of weeds and snakes. . . . Ho-hum!'

Demetrius had yawned, too, and wished they would go to bed.

'But it will be somebody else's turn, soon,' said Paulus.

'When?' asked Marcellus, exactly as Demetrius thought he might.

'Well, if justice were served to crazy old Tiberius and his addled stepchild,' deliberated Paulus, 'I should think it might be someone else's turn to-morrow—or by the end of next week, at the least. . . . How about a little more wine, Tribune?'

Demetrius had sat up, ready for the summons. It came instantly, and he presented himself.

'Fill Centurion Paulus's cup,' ordered Marcellus. 'No, none for me.'

And then Demetrius had gone back into the shadow of the tent to resume his waiting. The conversation had taken a queer turn now.

'Paulus,' his master was saying, 'you believe that the gods are manu-
factured by men. If it isn't an impertinent question, did you ever try
to make one?'

Demetrius, sauntering to-day along through a narrow ravine, almost
oblivious of the long procession single-filing on ahead, laughed as he
recalled that extraordinary question and its absurd answer.

'No,' Paulus had replied, 'but it isn't too late. Shall I make one for
you now?'

'By all means!' chuckled Marcellus. 'I assume that when you have
him completed he will closely resemble yourself.'

'Well—not too closely; for this god I'm going to invent is good. He
doesn't just pretend to be good. He really is good! He takes a few
bright men into his confidence—not necessarily Romans or Greeks or
Gauls; so long as they're honest and intelligent—and entrusts them with
some important tasks. He tells one man how to cure leprosy, and others
how to restore sight to the blind and hearing to the deaf. He confides
the secrets of light and fire; how to store up summer heat for use in
winter; how to capture the light of day and save it to illumine the
night; how to pour idle lakes on to arid land.' Paulus had paused,
probably to take another drink.

'Very good, Centurion,' Marcellus had commented, thoughtfully. 'If
you'll set up your god somewhere, and get him to producing these
effects, he can have all my trade.'

'Perhaps you might like to assist in his creation, sir,' suggested
Paulus, companionably.

Demetrius had not expected the quite serious speech that followed.
As it proceeded, he raised himself on one elbow and listened intently.

'It occurs to me, Paulus,' Marcellus was saying, soberly, 'that thi
god of yours, who seems a very fine fellow indeed, might well conside
a revision of the present plan for removing men from this worl
What happens to us is something like this: a man spends his activ
life striving to accomplish a few useful deeds, and eventually arrive
at the top of his powers; honoured—we will say—and a good exampl
to his community. Then he begins to go into a decline; loses his
teeth and his hair; his step slows, his eyes grow dim, his hearing is
dulled. This disintegration frets him, and he becomes gusty and
irascible, like an old dog. Now he retires to a sunny corner of the
garden with a woollen cap and a rug around his legs, and sits there
in everybody's way until it is time for him to take to his bed, with
grievous aches and pains which twist him into revolting postures.
When no dignity is left to him, nor any longer deserved, he opens his
sunken mouth and snores for a few days, unaware of his inglorious end.

Now, I think your new god should do something about this, Paulus.'
'We will discuss it with him, sir,' promised Paulus, agreeably. 'How would you like to have the matter handled?'

Apparently this required some concentration, for the reply was delayed a little while. When it came, Marcellus's tone had abandoned all trace of persiflage and was deeply sincere.

'When a Roman of our sort comes of age, Paulus, there is an impressive ceremony by which we are inducted into manhood. Doubtless you felt, as I did, that this was one of the high moments of life. Well do I remember—the thrill of it abides with me still—how all our relatives and friends assembled, that day, in the stately Forum Julium. My father made an address, welcoming me into Roman citizenship. It was as if I had never lived until that hour. I was so deeply stirred, Paulus, that my eyes swam with tears. And then good old Cornelius Capito made a speech, a very serious one, about Rome's right to my loyalty, my courage, and my strength. I knew that tough old Capito had a right to talk of such matters, and I was proud that he was there! They beckoned to me, and I stepped forward. Capito and my father put the white toga on me—and life had begun!'

There was an interval of silence here. Demetrius, much moved by this recital, had strained to hear above his own accented heart-beats, for the reminiscence had been spoken in a tone so low that it was almost as if Marcellus were talking to himself.

'Now, I think your god should ordain that at the crowning moment of a mature man's career; at the apex; when his strength has reached its zenith; when his best contribution has been made; let your god ordain that another assembly be held, with all present who know and revere this worthy man. And who among us would not strive to be worthy, with such a consummation in prospect? Let there be a great assembly of the people. Let there be an accounting of this man's deeds; and, if he has earned a lofty eulogy, let it be spoken with eloquence.'

'And then?' demanded Paulus. 'A valedictory, perhaps?'

'No,' Marcellus had decided, after a pause. 'Let the man keep silent. He will have no need to explain his deeds, if they were worth emulation. He will arise, and his peers will remove his toga; and it will be treasured, perhaps conferred upon another, some day, for courageous action. It would be a great responsibility to wear such a garment, Paulus.' There was another long pause.

'I think the god should prescribe that this event occur in the waning of a golden afternoon in springtime. There should be a great chorus, singing an elegiac ode. And while the triumphant music fills the air—with the vast assembly standing reverently—let the honoured man

march erectly and with firm step from the rostrum,
the sunset! Then—let him vanish! And be seen no m

After he had gone to bed, last night, and the camp
for the footfalls and jangling side-arms of the sentri
pondered long and deeply over this strange conceit—
better god!

This morning, as he marched through the barren l
of stupid donkeys who had as much control over their
over his own, Demetrius wondered what he might
had invited him to add a desirable attribute to their
Doubtless the world would be a more comfortable p
as Paulus had suggested, some plan were arrived at
tribution of light and heat. And perhaps it would b
to a more dramatic conclusion if, as his master h
visioned, the human career might close with musi
instead of a tedious glissade into helpless senility;
stood, a man's lack of honour at the end of his life s
patible with his absurd plight at life's beginning. If M
to add dignity to a man's departure from the world, h
or a more dignified arrival.

No, such idle speculations were a mere waste of o
had a chance to mend the world. There were other n
import. Surely, this amazingly honest deity whor
Paulus had invoked would want to do something
injustice of men in their dealings one with another.
tion, Demetrius reconstructed the painful scene of
Roman ruffians forced the doors, and threw his beau t
as they stalked into his honoured father's library t
carry him away to his death.

This nobler god—if he had any interest in justic
appear, at such a tragic moment, and sternly declar
that!'

Demetrius repeated the words aloud—over and o
louder—until the high-walled ravine believed in
so.

'*You can't do that!*' he shouted, so loudly that Melas
turned to look back inquiringly.

* * * * * *

They had all but reached the end of their journey no
hour their caravan had been plodding up a long hill. A
impressive spectacle had confronted them. They w